BLUE LAND

Also by C. D. Collins

Kentucky Stories (1999)

Subtracting Down (2004)

Carousel Lounge (2008)

Self-Portrait With Severed Head (2008)

Kentucky native C. D. Collins has published short fiction in numerous literary journals, including *StoryQuarterly*, *The Pennsylvania Review*, *Salamander* and *Phoebe*. With funds from the St. Botolph Club Foundation, Harvard University, the Cambridge Arts Council and the Somerville Arts Council, she has produced three award-winning compact discs of spoken-word with music. Ms. Collins has performed widely at such venues as Berklee College of Music, Boston's Institute of Contemporary Art and Club Passim. Her lyric documentary, *Understory*, which chronicles the environmentally devastating practice of mountaintop removal to retrieve Appalachian coal, may be viewed at www.cdcollins.com. Ms. Collins lives in Massachusetts and Kentucky with her notorious movie-star cats.

This is a work of fiction. Names, characters, places and incidents are either the product of the author's imagination or are used ficticiously. Any resemblance to actual persons, living or dead, business establishments, events or locales, is entirely coincidental.

Text set in Centaur at Polyho Press

Cover photo © John Chervinsky

First Trade Edition

ISBN-13: 978-0-9771557-2-9

Polyho Press
10 Howard Street
Somerville, Massachusetts 02144
www.polyho.com

BLUE LAND

stories

C. D. Collins

Polyho Press • Somerville, Massachusetts

For

Lula and Babette

&

My Familiars

Fact explains nothing. On the contrary, it is fact that requires explanation.

— Marilynne Robinson, *Housekeeping*

The Vigilantes of Vance

WHEN I WAS FIVE, I stood in the front seat of the car while my mother speeded down country lanes and careened around blind curves on the wrong side of the road. She drove with one foot on the accelerator, the other on the brake, cup of coffee in one hand, cigarette in the other, and never once used a turn signal. At that time, the speed limit was seventy-five, which Kentucky motorists regarded as a "suggested average," even on the winding pikes, branches, runs and levees. No one had ever heard of child restraints, designated drivers or secondary smoke.

Winter mornings, the Buick's interior filled with the mingling incense of filterless Pall Malls and Chanel No. 5. The car climbed steep grades with the ease of a panther. My mother, with her untamed blond hair and fox jacket, was like a beautiful wild animal, too, unpredictable, preoccupied with missions I could scarcely comprehend. I regarded her from a distance—the dark brows above intent violet eyes, the small full mouth—never knowing when she might strike.

The moment it was warm enough to drive with the top down my mother and I took twenty-mile detours home from shopping, topping the mountain crests and sailing into the lengthening dusk devouring light bread, spice drop candy and entire quarts of blueberries. We'd pull into our driveway, blue-lipped and exhilarated, the family dogs rushing the car, scratching its glossy red paint. The dogs were immensely relieved to see my mother, as though they'd been holding their breath the whole time we'd been gone. I'd lose her then: to the dogs, to my father and brother, whose faces appeared behind the screen door like gibbous moons. We'd unpack the groceries, fill the blue satin-glass candy dish with the remaining spice drops, and make dinner.

My mother's dogs, spoiled to the point of hysteria, followed her from room to room with wet, fearful eyes, lest she escape again. They sat at her feet when she played the piano, singing as close to the melody as they could get.

The family hierarchy positioned dogs far above cats, which were relegated to the outdoors. I'd find my kittens on the road, their eye roots bulged out like diced potatoes, then bury them in shoe boxes with creek rocks for headstones. My parents seemed to regard cats as having the loose morals of Locust Street floozies who shimmied up to men on bar stools down at Hozay's. As punishment for their wanton reproduction, my parents drove my mamma cats out into the country and "dropped them off."

It's not like my parents never visited Locust Street. I'd wait for my mother in the car outside Hozay's while she went inside to look for my father. I'd stare at the sign for Kentucky Utilities, the neon man with the bolt of electricity in his hand, which blinked off and on—REDDY KILOWATT: YOUR ELECTRIC SERVANT. I'd test how close I could get the cigarette lighter's red coil to my skin before it singed. It seemed like hours since my mother had gone in there, her Derringer plucked from the glove compartment and dropped into her purse, casually, like a roll of mints.

At home, my brother and I listened to the continuing argument from the basement, where we read Archie comic books, smoked cigarettes and sniffed gasoline from the lawn mower can. "I trust that woman about as far as I can throw her," my mother shouted. "Which ain't very damn far."

Their feet shifted back and forth above our heads.

"You're stepping out on me."

"Like hell. *You* are."

Stop! I wanted to shout.

They were both right, I found out, later, after I'd moved away from home to the relative safety of inner-city Boston. My parents divorced, my brother started his own family, and my mother turned the corner about cats. Now she's the one who takes in strays, naming them after men she considers strong-minded—Louis Farrakhan, Khomeini, and her favorite, Hussein, a black Persian she has nicknamed Hootie to avoid his being shot by the neighbors.

"*Hooo*-tie!" she calls out the back door. She'd found him by the side of the road with one of his little legs broken. "Somebody must have thrown him out their car," she says, as though she can hardly fathom such a thing.

Each spring, I cross seven states, south and west, each state larger, greener, less populated, than the one before, straight through till I arrive on my mother's doorstep. Mornings, we tour her flower garden. She wears her silk robe and walks slowly, sipping coffee from a chipped Haviland china cup. I follow her past the last of the Black Parrot tulips, down treacherous cinder-block stairs. Columbine and Lilies-of-the-Valley bloom on either side.

"I seduced Reverend Grayson last Sunday," she tells me.

"You seduced a gay preacher?" I ask.

"Well, see this little patch of Columbines, how their blooms are about four times as big as the others? They must be mutants. So, I took one down to the Episcopal church and asked Reverend Grayson if his Columbines were as big as my Columbines and he said, 'Pearl, if you're not doing anything this afternoon, I'd sure like to come by and see your garden.'"

Overnight, three new irises have bloomed. They must be mutants too, because each flower is roughly the size of a St. Bernard's head. "This is Streetwalker," she tells me, pointing to deep amethyst flower with a scarlet center. "Isn't she just a show-off?" She removes all two-day old blossoms, claiming that they look like used condoms.

At the bottom of the steps, Oriental Poppies weigh heavily on their stems, vermilion petals flung open to reveal spokes peppered in purple soot. "I'd love to get the opium out of those," she tells me. "Wonder what the recipe is."

Smiling, she looks suddenly like herself at twenty-eight,

her expression delighted as she floored the accelerator on the Jaguar she'd insisted on buying even though she had to wrap its engine in a blanket at night to get it to start. It seems that my mother has not so much aged as collected faces, which emerge and recede depending on her mood and the story she's telling.

My mother has been vice-president of the Clay County Humane Society for three years. The President, Miss Lucille, a blue-haired woman in her seventies, whose buttermilk biscuits win the blue ribbon at the fair every year; the Secretary, Tom Richmond, whose charm melts the hearts of all the unmarried women in town, who in turn maintain a collective denial about the existence of Tom's boyfriend; and my mother, who has been known to attend Humane Society meetings in her fox jacket: these three form a triumvirate, a kind of little mafia, intent and ruthless in their mission.

Last week, Miss Lucille put a brick through the windshield of a car in the Kroger parking lot in order to give the dog inside some air. She left a message reading, *Please crack your window.*

Spring in Kentucky arrives six weeks earlier than "spring" in New England. In April, it's warm enough to stretch out on the tattered chaise beside my mother's algae-ridden pool and angle our faces toward the sun. The pool's water is the same temperature as a sunny New England bay on the hottest August afternoon: too cold for swimming. I think how the ecology of my mother's house and yard has become fragile over the years, its operation and maintenance just at the limit of her budget and determination to keep up with it.

"I've got to vacuum this pool," she says, as though to echo my thoughts, though she makes no move to do so and neither do I. Instead, she takes a long drag from her cigarette, neglecting to exhale the smoke.

"I don't like that Hillary Clinton," she says.

"Well, that's predictable," I say.

"I know what you think," my mother says, "You think I favor the men and slight the women, don't you?"

"Yes," I answer, unsure where this might lead.

"You're right," she says. "It's just that growing up, I always looked to the men to protect me."

"What man ever protected you?"

Instead of answering, she invites me for a drive to the Lexington Cemetery to see the weeping cherries. I volunteer to drive my car, hoping to prevent her from smoking. She inhales one last puff before getting in, then exhales, filling the interior with smoke.

The weeping cherries in the cemetery fill our field of vision. The blossoms cascade from the treetops, pink and white waterfalls on either side of our path.

"You know," my mother said, "last year when Prince died I was burying him in the back yard and your father just appeared over by the fence. It was almost dark and at first all I could see was one of those pressed white shirts like he always wears. Didn't say a word, just took the shovel and finished digging the hole."

I missed going home for spring this year, but everyone said it was cold and that the frost caught the fruit trees and froze their blossoms off.

I called on Derby night, but my mother wasn't home. So I called again on Sunday.

"Where were you last night?" I ask. In our family, it would be considered overly formal to introduce oneself over the telephone, even if you haven't spoken to the person in years.

"At a party down at Tom and Dave's," my mother says. "I took that bottle of tequila that your friend Maria gave me."

"Amelia," I say.

"That's it, Amelia. I can't remember anything anymore. Anyway, I mixed the tequila with peach juice."

"That sounds horrible," I say.

"Well, that's what Reverend Grayson said. But the bunch of drunks drank it anyway, didn't they? Then we started in on Tom's mint juleps."

"Who all was there?" I ask her.

"Just Tom and Dave and Father Grayson and Mary Lou Bishop and her friend. Mary Lou said that since her husband died—you know he laid up in that house for years, we thought he was going to outlive us all—but now she says she's going to rent a villa in Italy and invite us all over."

"Has Mary Lou come out yet," I ask her.

"Mary Lou is not a lesbian."

"Mom ..."

"Now, she might lead a lesbian lifestyle ..."

"You mean like butch her hair and golf at the country club?"

"Right."

"And live with a woman whose voice is on the answering machine."

"How did you know that?"

"You're not the only one with sources," I say. I picture the Derby party in Tom's impeccably arranged living room on Sycamore Street, the five gay people left in Vance gathered around my mother as though she were Marlene Dietrich resurrected in her finest hour.

"What were you doing when I called?" I ask her.

"Eating a piece of candy."

"I caught you, didn't I?"

"Yes, you did."

"What kind of candy?"

"It's a spice drop. Yesterday, I had a hankering for a spice drop and had to go to two stores before I found them."

"Where did you find them?"

"Kroger."

I can almost taste one of the bright domes, encased in sugar crystals, melting on my tongue.

Monkey Alley

My GRANDFATHER, Whitley Enoch, was a handsome, impatient man with a confident gait and what my mother called "good bones."

He married his second wife, Cat, and moved into the house on her big farm out in Cream Alley, a section of the county known for its dairy cows. He sired four kids, one after the other, and settled into his jobs as rural-route mail carrier in the morning, a ceramic artist in the afternoon.

James and I didn't give a solitary damn about our grandfather. We preferred his ex-wife, our California Granny, who lived a magical life out in Los Angeles. Sometimes she sent us shuffleboard games and pink grapefruits for Christmas, and sometimes she forgot all about the holidays.

Our step-grandmother Cat was a farmer and an elementary school teacher, who seemed think Whitley was some kind of royalty. She never said his name, only "Him."

"I'll just sit in back beside Him," she'd say, pressing the

button on the car door handle and swinging it open with her tiny hands. When she dressed up, Cat pulled on white leather gloves with an iris cut out on each wrist. She wore gabardine skirts and cashmere sweaters, shoes hand-made in Italy. She'd slide in, clutching her enormous pocketbook and smiling like she'd arrived in the Promised Land. No matter what she did to get close to him, Whitley would just look the other way.

Whitley strode to the barn in linen pants and a straw fedora, proud as one of his fighting cocks. I watched him shelling hard corn as his roosters paced ravenously in their cages. They pecked their food in staccato rhythm, ruffling their iridescent feathers and darting their gold sociopathic eyes.

Your real wife ran off and left you, didn't she, mister, I thought to myself. *You're not such a hot shot.*

Whitley and Cat's three girls, Nell, Jerky and Lacey all lived in one room. Whitley Jr., whose name got condensed to Lee, had a room all to himself. None of the girls were allowed in there, including me and even James, since he was a kid.

A gangly, freckled teenaged girl named Maggie lived there, too. She cooked and cleaned and slept on a cot in the hallway that led to the sun room where Whitley practiced violin. According to Nell, Maggie's life was now a good deal better than it used to be. She'd been the eldest child in a family with a dozen kids who ate nothing but biscuits with gravy and commodity cheese.

Maggie also assisted Whitley with his porcelain ceramics, which required precise brush-work with colored paints and glazes. She amazed everyone with her 40/20 eyesight, which meant she could see at forty feet what most people can see at twenty. When she finished a piece, Whitley picked it up and examined it—the delicate eyebrows and pink lips on the figures, the fine scroll work on the cream pitchers, and the intricate feathering on the ceramic birds. If he set it back down without a word, it meant that he approved.

Lee was the oldest of Whitley and Cat's kids. Nell was the youngest, and my favorite. Even though she was our aunt, she was only a year older than James. Her hair was soft and straight as dental floss, and even her summer skin was the translucent blue of skimmed milk. Jerky was the pretty one, dark-haired and quiet, the one Whitley took to town for ice cream. Lacey, the peacemaker, had strange habits, like tithing her allowance and saving bits of her dinner for the little shrine on her dresser.

"Nell's got the shape," Cat said, protectively. "She won't have any trouble with the men." Whitley barely claimed Nell because she looked like Cat, not him. He held people responsible for their lot, as though being poor, ill or ugly were choices people made.

One June morning, my parents headed to Keenland race track and dropped James and I off in Cream Alley. The kids had already set up the front yard for croquet, so we rocked on the glider while they finished knocking the bright wooden balls through all the wickets. Games were serious business with the Enochs.

When it was my turn, I picked the green mallet. We could choose whatever color we wanted except red. Lee owned anything red. We whacked the battered balls through the hot, wet grass until we got tired and started cheating.

"Punks," Lee muttered to himself. We weren't worth addressing directly. He slid his mallet back into its caddie with malicious precision. "Punk babies." He went back to painting on the side of his Ford Falcon.

Lee wouldn't allow us inside, so we ogled the dashboard's fur trim and gearshift knob fashioned from a red number seven pool ball. He wrote "C-a-n-" in flowing gold script on the right front fender.

"Candy Man," Nell whispered in my ear. She smelled of earth and the new perfume Lee was developing called "Date Bait."

Lee shot Nell a warning look. *Come on,* she mouthed. We followed her around the house to the sun room. On the patio, a bronze boot snap had been anchored into the cement. The snap was shaped like a woman with her hands behind her head and her legs spread in the air. If you hooked your foot between her legs, she yanked your shoe off. Whitley had a whole collection of nasty things in his sun room, too, an ashtray with a bare-breasted lady, her ceramic legs swung from a tiny wire at her hips; a cast-iron Aunt Jemima, who opened pop bottles with her teeth.

Nell used a skeleton key to open a glass cabinet lined with violins. She unsnapped the felt-lined case and laid one on the table. We admired the dark, swirling wood of the back.

"Bird's-eye maple," Nell said. Nell knew everything. Running my fingers along the horsehair bow, I noticed that one direction was smooth, the other rough. A white, sticky powder that smelled of pine rubbed off on my fingers. James held the violin at each end and I drew the bow over the strings.

A trembling note rose into the air and I thought for a moment that I'd broken something.

As she was returning the violin to its case, we heard the door click shut. Before we could run, Lee had grabbed Nell's arm and twisted it behind her back.

"Thief," Lee hissed. "Ugly slut thief." He spun Nell around. "Close your eyes," he commanded. Gripping her around the waist with one arm, he pressed her eyes with the thumb and forefinger of the other hand, bearing down till I thought her eyeballs would burst. Nell's trembling hands cupped the air around Lee's hand as if it were a candle she was protecting from the wind. She was completely silent.

"Good," he said, letting go and thrusting her away. "You're getting better. Now straighten up this room before Dad sees it."

Maggie called to us and we fled to the kitchen. Lee was the general, Nell explained, she, his soldier. He was building her courage and resistance to pain. Sometimes, Lee made Nell stand against the barn like a woman on a roulette wheel, while he threw handmade darts constructed from matchsticks and sewing needles. If Nell flinched, she had to do Lee's chores. If she was brave, she got points. A hundred points, Lee would take her for a ride in the "Candy Man."

Maggie was sitting on her stool next to the stove, smoking a Pall Mall. "If you all want a cobbler, best pick me some blackberries," she said. The cigarette hung from the corner of her mouth as she tied leather chaps on James and me. Nell wore her flannel-lined corduroy pants.

"Careful, hear?" Maggie said, handing us each a clean lard pail. "Horseflies and snakes like berries, too. So don't go grabbing in where you can't see, and step light." Maggie squinted through the smoke to survey the chaps. She crushed her cigarette out in a ceramic hand and shooed us out of the kitchen.

The gate creaked as we crept into the garden. We pressed it shut and tiptoed around till we found three perfect tomatoes.

"I got some salt out of the sheds," Nell said, showing us the white crumbling pyramid in the bottom of her blue bandanna. She dropped the ripe tomatoes on top of it and tied the bandanna into a sack. Nell only liked vegetables, but at the table she was forced to eat meat. We had stolen Pall Malls from Maggie's pack.

Whitley cured his own hams. He considered every part of the pig a delicacy: the blood, the feet, the brains, the snout. He made souse meat, which he kept refrigerated in colossal jars of gray and green masses with flecks of red.

In the field beyond the barn, we found the thorny blackberry stalks along the fence line. Above the blackberry briars, wild roses and honeysuckle crested in a tangled wave over our heads enveloping us in a moist fragrant cloud. James and I picked the berries one at a time, plunking them into our buckets. Nell's hands were small and nimble, like her mother's; she could pull five or six berries off in a clump without mashing them.

She glanced into our buckets. "It's okay to get a few red ones, it makes the pie tart. Just try not to get the stems." She kissed our purple-tipped fingers like they were precious jewels.

All our aunts made a big deal about James and me, wanting us to sit in their laps and saving up their candy. They brushed our sandy hair that turned to burnished gold in summer. Our dark, heavy eyebrows gave an impression of seriousness, they said. All I could see was a chubby little girl who was shorter than everyone I knew except actual babies. To me, James was just a brat with skinny legs and clownish flaps of ears.

After an hour of picking, we were sweaty and itchy and ready to quit. We had more than enough berries, so we pulled off our overshirts and tied them around the tops of the buckets.

"Let's go to Monkey Alley!" James shouted. Nell looked dubious but she put the pails in the crook of a silver maple tree and we started racing each other. We just weren't supposed to go that close to the river, especially during deer season. Plus, by the time we crossed Shaker Creek, we'd be trespassing.

We hiked on down toward the creek in the steaming air while Nell told us Alfred Hitchcock stories. One was about a little white girl who never played with her doll because it was colored. In the end, the little colored doll changed into a real girl and that white girl changed into a little white doll that got left lying in the rain.

The thought of the little white girl trapped inside a doll spooked us and we took off across a deep field of alfalfa, then wound through the green corridors of a corn patch that was pollinating itself in the wind. "The corn's tasseling," Nell said, slowing to a walk, and pointing to fuzzy seeds that stuck to the green silks sprouting from the ends of the young ears. She pressed a finger to her lips. "Do not disturb."

We passed silently through the corn patch. Nell stretched out the barbed wire with her foot and hands so James and I could get through, then followed us. We were on Ballard's property now. Nell stopped on top of a hill and spread her white arms. "There's a breeze here, feel?" James and I mimicked her, holding our hands loosely in the air, swaying back and forth in the humid air. Then Nell dropped down the hill at a dead gallop and we followed, collapsing into the clover. After she got up and brushed off her shorts, she plucked a stalk of buck horn plantain, twisted the stem around the head and shot it into the air. "A few more furlongs, little fillies," she announced.

Monkey Alley was a row of Osage orange trees originally planted as a fence to keep cows out of the tobacco. There were no cows anymore and some of the trees had been cut down for fence posts. But some still stood as a fragment of a fortress in a thicket of smaller bushes and saplings. At the end of the row, the ground rose into a meadow of violets and purple clover. The largest Osage fed on the stream that ran before it. The grand old tree dominated the rise, its branches lying wide and thick, its roots creeping out in unpredictable tangles. When we reached the monkey tree, we could hear the river. If we stood on the roots, we could see through the thickets to the place where the land dropped off into a steep cliff down to the Kentucky River, old and deep, flanked by limestone palisades. We always acted wild when we got this far, fought with sticks and peed outside. I was always Robin Hood or Swamp Fox.

"Look at the monkey tree," Nell cried. James and I dropped our sticks, our chests heaving, and peered up into the dense, knotty branches. "Monkeys moving!" We stared. Monkeys seemed to crawl up the limbs, posing, chasing each other, their arms, legs and tails twisting together.

"Okay, close your eyes," Nell said. "Now open them."

We looked again and the monkeys were still. Then they were crawling again. It appeared that one turned its wooden head and gazed at me with vacant, carved eyes.

"Look at this mess they made," Nell exclaimed. The ground around the tree was covered with rough green balls the size of grapefruits. "Brain fruit," she said and pretended to take a bite.

We each settled into our root pockets at the base of the old tree and picked at the dirt, worn out, half listening to the urgent whispers of the old river. The squirrels hurried about, as lightweight as birds, sitting up, arching their tails into question marks or leaping across the tree crowns. I'd found a dead one once, uncollected by a hunter, and nudged it with my foot. I was surprised by its heaviness, its thick-waisted body, muscular and mute.

Nell unwrapped the tomatoes and we ate them in hungry, sucking bites, pressing the red flesh into the coarse salt of the opened bandanna. Then she pulled out two Pall Malls, struck a kitchen match on a slate rock and lit one of them. She inhaled and blew the smoke out in a thin column.

"I'm moving," she said. She handed the cigarette to James.

James took one draw and handed it to me. Maggie would miss three, we figured. So we kept our take down to one or two.

"Where to?" I asked, impressed. Moving was an indication of change and change always suggested something better. To my mind, smart people did a lot of moving.

"Don't know yet," Nell said. She picked a strand of tobacco off the end of her tongue and rolled it between her fingers.

I thought of my room at home at the back of the house where I lay awake refining my plans for various crises. One plan was to lie perfectly still when the burglars came through the window and stepped on my bed. Same thing with Jack the Ripper. I practiced slowing down my breathing, like those monks who trained their bodies so they could survive for days underground. I'd be absolutely still. They'd never see me.

"You could stay with me," I said.

"No," Nell said. My chest stung.

"They'd know where she was then, stupid," James rolled his eyes straight up, showing only the dark blue lower arcs of his irises, the whites beneath.

"How come you want to run away?" James asked.

"I'm in the way," Nell said. "It would make things easier on Mom, too," she said. Neither James nor I knew how to challenge that.

Under the monkey tree I was destroying a small branch, stripping its leaves and dragging it back and forth in the dirt. "Is it Lee bothering you?" I asked. I began breaking the branch into small sticks.

"No, Lee's all right," she said in that soft, direct way she had. "It's Dad."

I thought Lee belonged in prison. Every family had its own rules, its own stopping place, but it didn't seem that Lee had a stopping place. During dinners at the Enoch house, I watched his slim, smug face and pointed jaw working sidewise on the best pieces of meat, the biggest slices of pie. Nell sometimes cried at the dinner table, silently. No one ever asked why. In Kennedy's field, I knew of a walnut grove that backed up to a shelf of rock with a shallow cave. I could bring her food and water. No one would know. In the evenings I'd walk to the fields, and there in her plaid shorts and cotton shirts, her wide leathery feet, would be Nell, to take my hand.

The rough bark of the tree scraped and dirtied her thin blouse patterned with tiny faded daisies. "You know that new Chrysler we got last month?" she said, confidentially. "Well, it ain't so new now. Dad was firing some Wedgwood dishes one night in his new electric kiln and it was cooling too fast. The dishes just kept exploding. We all sat around nervous and then in a minute we'd hear another one, all soft, like cracking eggs. It was awful. Jerky and I were afraid we'd laugh if we looked at each other, so we just kept our books in front of us. Well, you know my Dad has sugar and he's not supposed to eat anything sweet.

"Maggie makes saccharin pies for him but sometimes he eats ours, anyway, which puts him in a mood. He ate two pieces of butterscotch meringue, one after the other. Suddenly he grabbed up all the glazes that Maggie had spread out on the table and ran outside and smeared them all over the hood of the Chrysler," Nell stopped a minute to finish up the cigarette and bury the coal. "But that wasn't enough," she continued, her voice rising. "No, he runs back in and gets some white high-gloss oil paint and a pint of Lee's Candy Apple Red and just flat covers the top. Us girls were up all night getting it off while it was still wet."

"How did you get it off?" James said.

"Turpentine. Took the gloss right off it, too. Look in around the windshield wipers when we get back," Nell said. "There's a dozen different colors."

I was thinking about all those colors and the long walk home for cobbler, when we heard a *zing* and a *thunk*. James clutched at his chest as some buckshot fell into the leaves in a small shower. Our jaws dropped. My heart kicked in my chest. James instantly pulled off his T-shirt to reveal a white line across his chest. It began to ooze red. Nell's blanched skin seemed to wax over and dark circles appeared under her eyes, her forehead rose in terror.

"Hey!" we heard a man's voice yelling. "Come back here. Hey! You kids okay?"

We didn't stop until we got back to the creek, pitching ourselves to the edge gulping air. I was picturing James's funeral. Everyone walking by the casket, then looking at me. The bottom seemed to fall out of my life like the trap floor in the giant spinning wooden bowl at Fountain Ferry. I would either drop through the bottom or fly out the top too light for gravity. "Little old buckshot grazed you, honey" Nell said. "You're going to be fine." Nell rubbed James's chest clean with the bandanna and creek water, then hid the soiled cloth beneath some brush.

"That was Clyde Ballard," Nell said, "He'll tell Dad, and Dad will wear me out."

We picked ourselves up and dragged homeward, retrieving the lard buckets on the way. It must have been very late because it was still high summer and the sun was already low and gold in the trees along the horizon.

Back home, we handed the blackberries over to Maggie.

"How long did you leave these a settin'?" looking suspiciously at the soupy contents of the buckets.

"We went wading in the creek for a while," Nell lied.

Maggie fussed with the berries over the sink. She could normally divine everything that happened. But tonight she betrayed nothing, so her complaints about the blackberries comforted us. Maggie had a special way of fixing everything. When she sliced tomatoes, she peeled them; she ground down coarse salt in a mortar for the butter and cottage cheese. Her blackberry cobblers and cream pies were known throughout the county.

Everyone slowly gathered in the kitchen while Maggie put the bowls on the table. Lacey and Jerky were fooling with a small black plastic box with strips of colored cardboard inside. Bible verses were printed on the strips to memorize. Lee had on a white shirt and khaki pants ready for his Saturday night date. He squeaked his chair when he sat down, arrogant and self-conscious. "Jesus wept," he said when it was his turn to recite a verse.

Cat sat in her cane-bottomed chair, reading her paper, Whitley surrounded by his implored Chihuahuas at the other. He occasionally dropped them scraps of fat or a hardened tip of meat.

After supper, Nell, James and I sat out on the stoop. Dusk hazed the hills into soft blue and the distant mountains looked like mounds of smoke. In the half-light, Nell's image wavered before my eyes. I had always thought she was a mix between the way I wanted my mother to be and Davy Crockett, but tonight I saw her differently. She was no different from James and me, little nervous kids pulling at the grass.

Nell was not really going to move. It was just talk, like

all those old stories she told us. She wasn't going anywhere. James sat hunched over the stoop touching lightly underneath his shirt. The Chrysler hulked in the drive. I thought about going over to look under the wipers for the paint, but it was probably too dark to see.

Household Ghosts

It was the dream of Harley Coleman to see to it that both his sons, Earl and Jake, had their own house before he died. The three men worked evenings, weekends, all through scorching, hazy-skied summer days, then stopped by the home farm for one of Beaulah May's dinners: bowls heaped with her garden's produce, creamed, minced, pickled, skillet-fried; two meats, iced tea in pitchers, real shortcake with strawberries dark and bright as nodding hearts.

By the time they finished Earl's house out on the Levee, Harley was thinning; half-way through Jake's on Mercer's Landing, he was having cold sweats. Still, Harley worked past dusk, siding the house in gray shingle, rolling out tar sheets on the roof. "You don't cut corners if you aim to do it right."

When Beaulah May and Harley sold the home farm and moved in with Jake, there were three kids for Beaulah May to teach how to string half-runner beans, how to punch holes in the top of their beetle-collecting jars, and to entertain with stories about her little sister, Goldie, who died of scarlet fever.

"Children, I see her floating around the house, a wispy gentian blue. That was the color of the little dress she was buried in."

"Do you see Jesus, too?" Katie asked, her eyes wide as a bobcat's. Katie was the one with all the questions.

Beaulah May studied the children's faces, dumped another bag of Silver Queen onto the rough boards. "I've seen him of a morning, strolling in the garden."

When Beaulah May turned the pages of the picture books at the library, she understood that the painters back then truly walked among spirits. She studied the weight and density of the bodies of mortal men who ate dates and drank cool well water. How clearly those painters saw even the shimmering flesh of angels who cleaved the sky in two. All she saw of Goldie was a trail of dress disappearing around the corner like she was still twelve years old, playing with Beaulah May like she used to. Even her Jesus never came close, only smiled at her over by the Sweet Pea vines, so vaporous she could practically see through him.

She always wanted to behold those paintings first-hand, in places like Washington D.C., or Rome, or London, England. Beaulah May supposed it was harder to see God's Son and His angels as time went on. It had been two thousand years. People forget.

Harley died in his hickory chair one evening before they'd finished pointing up the chimney, so it was no surprise to Beaulah May that she heard him on the roof, tamping bricks in place with his hammer not two days after his own funeral.

It was a comfort to her, the tap tapping above her head as she cut out biscuit dough or put up peach preserves.

When Beaulah May took sick, she'd been living for five years in the new house that Earl had built right beside the old one. The boys were "contractors" now and drove trucks with COLEMAN BROTHERS painted on the sides in 14-karat gold. She had her own room with flocked wall paper and carpet so deep she could hardly walk on it. They didn't need her to help cook or clean because they'd hired a maid, and Earl's wife, who seemed to dote on carrot sticks, found Beaulah May's cooking too rich.

They sewed Beaulah May up just as soon as they cut her open. This was in the days when they didn't tell you a thing, but she figured it out when the family started visiting again and her skin turned yellow as meal.

Katie came down from college with her friends who played guitars and harmonicas and sang about how love and sorrow flow mingled down from the crown of Jesus.

"That's real pretty," Beaulah May said. She was thinking about the luster of their long hair in the sun and that she'd always wanted to learn the piano.

After her friends had driven off in their camouflage van, Katie asked her grandmother what she'd come to find out. "Do you ever see Grandpa?"

Beaulah May whispered, because Earl's wife had warned her against telling "ghost stories." She told Katie how Harley's hammering had got kindly frantic, how she didn't think it was fair to let him follow her to another house like Goldie had. So one day she took off her apron and said loud to be sure he'd hear her, "Harley, you can stop your hammering, now. The house is finished."

Beaulah May knew that when she left Earl's new house, nothing of her would remain. She sat back in her chair and listened as Katie played another song, an old one that pleased her, a chant or hymn from the time when they still remembered. She thought of the house where she'd join Harley again. She could see it. The house built with neither stone nor shingle. The house not built with hands.

Hiroshima

It was so hot that she and her grandmother had rolled up the wool rugs and put down straw mats. They'd shuttered the house into deep shade. It was August and in the long afternoon, her grandparents were napping, as they did every day at four. She sat on the porch combing her just-washed hair, her feet propped on the strong gray railing.

Downtown, a young man waited as Mr. Greenaway crossed the street in his straw fedora on his way to the dairy. The young man's arms were solid and covered with coarse hair. When he waved to Mr. Greenaway, this hair caught the still-high afternoon sun and reflected glints of auburn.

On the porch the air did not move. Here in her grandparents' house, nothing ever moved, only days of piano lessons and separating the lily roots in the flower garden or slow walks to the dairy for strawberry ice cream. She knew that the heat would submerge her grandparents in sleep until the sun slanted red and low at dusk.

She had bathed and powdered, strapped on her new sandals of soft leather. She had pulled her white eyelet dress down over her freckled, summer-browned skin.

Sometimes on these walks, the soles of her feet sensed the solid crust of the earth, which buoyed her, and beneath, how the rich soil floated on its mantle of molten nickel and basalt.

Sometimes in sleep she reached down into the dark marble of these deep spheres. When she wakened her hands were covered with reflecting bits of mica. On this day, she combed her long, wet hair, flicking drops of water which evaporated as they struck the gray wood.

Up Sycamore Street, another young man, wearing loose pleated trousers and his best white shirt, strode toward her. As he turned the corner, he began to hurry.

Her cells have a longing, a heat greater than the one that overwhelms and stills this town. A volcanic heat, unquiet, carried on her liquid voice. She has been daring, impulsive really, unable to decide between them. She thought of them as cool breezes that would lift her hair, breezes for whose caress she would bare her face. She thought of them as a long trip, all the way to the ocean, which she has never seen. She has a notion, a forethought or a memory, of a ride in a convertible through salt water marshes, breathing in the blue sea air, the astringent scent of the man beside her.

She'd met them both at the carnival, handsome and earnest in their uniforms, having just come home from the war. She was seventeen. It was Saturday, late August. She has made two dates.

Would it have been different if Mr. Greenaway had not been walking this way to the dairy, if the other young man's step had not quickened as the image of her eyes surfaced in his mind? For it was not much time, just a moment, between the arrival of one and the arrival of the other, leaving with one, and leaving the other with the grandparents or the empty porch. Would the child that comes later have been the same soul destined to pass through this woman? Or is there a child whose soul still waits?

They say that when the bomb dropped on Hiroshima that year, such a number of astral bodies rose at once that the Oversoul could not expand to accommodate them, that for years after, the countryside was haunted by their ghosts.

The girl on the porch, waiting, has little knowledge of the islands in that faraway ocean, of the volcanic ring of fire. But there is something in her from the earth's core. Her body holds the information, igneous, fire-formed, so it's not a question of how much knowledge she will acquire, but of what, on her journey, she will remember.

The child that comes will perhaps paint a picture, or write a poem, that holds a surface which will sound all the echoes of her mother. Especially the moment, when through the arch of the smooth-vined and lavender-blossomed wisteria, her mother had caught sight of the dark wavy hair and eyebrows like raven's wings of the fervent young man who was to become this child's father.

Hands

*A History of Kentucky Tobacco Farming
in Five Voices*

1944, *Clest Lanier*

I plow up land, harrow the soil till the texture's fine as sand. I broadcast seed, lay down sheets of gauze to protect the seedlings from frost. I stake the gauze.

At my kitchen table, I eat biscuits, gravy and home-made sausage with my wife, who is expecting. Her apron has a dark wet line where she's been leaning against the counter washing dishes. She's big. I'm thinking maybe a boy, tall and broad-shouldered as my brother in the service.

Four hands at this table, to fetch well water, draw overalls through the wringer washer, hang hams in the smokehouse to cure. Four hands, soon six.

I plant corn, soybeans, wheat, tobacco on half shares. Owner provides land; I provide labor, split the profit. Government counts every bushel. Too much corn, they cut you back to stabilize the price. Each farm is allowed to raise only so many pounds of tobacco.

After dinner, I stand on the porch of the tenant house, drinking coffee and thinking about farming with my brother when he gets back from overseas, God willing. About how I'll own my own farm someday.

I've already picked out a name—*Dove's Run. Owner: Clest Lanier.*

I look out over the ridge at the tobacco cloths glowing in the dusk. Underneath the cloths: tobacco seed, mustard greens and Bibb lettuce, three kinds of tomatoes. Inside, my wife marks off the day in the almanac: April 17, 1944.

The strips of gauze buck in the breeze like sails in a sea of new green wheat. I hope it comes a flood.

1954, *Drema Lanier*

It comes a flood. Every seed sprouts, every weed thrives. The plants bulge, stretching the cloths tight. I strip back the gauze, pull up the warm, furry-leafed plants, wrap their roots in wet newspaper. Me and my twin sister perch on the back of the tractor and feed the plants into the tobacco setter—it whirls like a little Ferris wheel, tucks each plant into a furrow and gives it a squirt of water.

Every day I set tobacco, every evening I carry buckets of water that bang against my knees, one tin cupful per plant.

Saturdays, me and my sister ride downtown in the back of our daddy's truck. We sit on a bench in front of the courthouse eating ice cream. I am nine. Sometimes my parents can't tell me and my sister Darla apart.

The men roll cigarettes in thin paper, and blue smoke

drifts toward me, smelling spicy and sweet. It's so hot you could grill a catfish on the storm drain. The only thing that saves me is this here ice cream cone, which I pretend I am eating on the Polar Express all the way to Alaska.

I half listen to the men talking about how the government has lifted the controls off corn, how farmers can raise as much as they want. My Uncle Lloyd, who left his trigger finger in France, says that's a good thing. Old man Sturgill's not so sure.

I know these men, their houses, yards and dogs because I sometimes ride with my father on his milk route. Wintertime, we're already back home by first light.

In July, plants shade me as I chop weeds from between the rows. My bare feet break up dirt clods. I can walk across a busted pop bottle without getting cut.

On television, there is a commercial showing dressed-up people at a party all lighting cigarettes. "Take a puff, it's springtime."

I have trouble in school because I always start the year late and because I spell words how they say them at home. Like *backer*, instead of tobacco, *hire*, instead of harrow.

Mama says I will have to buckle down.

1974, *Boone Taulbee*

I quit school early to plant. It's my senior year but me and my brothers have bought a six-row combine and leased out four hundred acres for corn and soybeans and beef cattle. My brothers and their wives all work factory shifts. Afternoons, my sister-in-law, Drema, works beside me. She used to have a twin sister. In pictures, you can't tell them apart to save your life. Drema's mad at me for quitting school.

Come August, I stride down the rows, breaking off the purple blossom clusters with my bare hands, left right, left right. Topping the tobacco, so the leaves can fill out and mature, green transforming into gold.

I harvest ten hours a day, six days a week, slicing the base of the stalk with my Tomahawk hatchet, sliding the plant over the metal spear onto a hickory stick. Four plants per stick, jam the spear onto the next stick and keep cutting. I work alongside my brothers, Elgin and Mason, proceeding down the long rows. Their slick brown backs bow forward in rhythm. With this work, you can't waste movement; you can't rush. A misplaced swing can slice off a toe, cleave a thigh clean to the bone. My eldest brother, Rudy, is supposed to help, but he's probably laying up in that shack down in Roan County. Vietnam changed him.

Farming has changed, too. Profits whittled so slim you've got to produce three, four times what you used to. You have to think big.

I'm the youngest, tallest, strongest boy in my whole family. At school, I could tackle two guys at a time, rebound a basketball half a county away. I can cut twenty rows of tobacco in a day, turn around and dance till the moon shouts, "Morning, glory!" Oh, hell yeah!

I heave the full sticks onto the wagon bed and ride rumbling behind the tractor to the barn where the hangers wait, women straddling the middle rungs, younger cousins three stories high scurrying along the maze of rails. Little monkeys. It's a whole new age, so say those girls in headbands and see-through blouses down at Rudy's cabin. My life spreads out ahead of me, a ribbon of joy.

1986, *Drema Lanier Taulbee*

My husband, Elgin, hands the stick up. I grab it, hoist it to a young one. Up and up till we pack the barn from the highest bent down, till the leaves brush the tops of our heads when we walk underneath.

Six weeks later, the tobacco is cured and a warm rain brings it into case. A moist leaf holds together when you strip it off the stalk. A dry leaf disintegrates in your hand. I lay a stalk on the long table, pull off the big bottom leaves, the flines and trash, pass it on to Carlos, who pulls off the middles, the lugs and brights, on to my husband who pulls off the tops, the reds, good for pipe and chewing tobacco. I rotate with the Mexicans, who are the only ones I can count on to work anymore. My husband is gruff today; misses his little brother Boone around stripping time.

Everybody knew Boone was up with that no 'count Rudy raising marijuana in the mountains. Boone had kept his head above water for ten years, laboring like an ox. The '84 drought hit him hard. Lost his crops, his jacked-up truck, little house out in Green Briar.

Damn corn. Brings the same $2.25 a bushel it brought twenty years ago with the price of everything else doubled. Nobody tries anymore. Not corn. Not soybeans. Not wheat. Lucky if you break even. Tobacco is the only legal cash crop left in this state, and thank God for it.

My hands work fast, my palms and fingernails stained mahogany from the leaves. My sister and mother had the same long, piano-player hands. Inside the stripping room, the rusty, homesick scent of tobacco makes the air dense.

I call for Carlos' wife to replace me on the line and step out of the barn into the evening mist. Beautiful crop this year. Clean and sweated. Gold type finish. Real pretty.

I fold a piece of gum into my mouth and wedge my hands into my jeans pockets, riding out an impulse to smoke. Last month, Dr. Fairchild passed around a slice of bad lung in a baggie for us morning-shift girls. "Looks like brown Swiss cheese, don't it?" Faye Ginter said and lit up with a strike-any-where match. But I left my Winstons right there on the cafeteria table.

That drought was only two years ago, the year I turned forty. I wonder what my life would have been if my sister Darla hadn't run off with that wild boy, if that sports car hadn't been a flying. Only nineteen. I've lived half my life with only half my self. That's how it seems. I sense her beside me though, always, that tender shadow.

I know my Dad is stripping tobacco in his barn out in Dove's Run, where the moist air is perfumed with Winesap apples and wood smoke. Our crop is scheduled for auction December 11, just in time to buy Christmas presents. I look out over the acres of harvested stalks, cut on the diagonal, like a field of bayonets.

1999, *Clest Lanier*

I stand at the December auction and they don't want my drought-stricken tobacco. Next year, they're talking about doing away with the quota system. Farmers can raise as much as they want. Then the companies will have all the power.

Phillip Morris contract you out for 100,000 pounds, leave out the little farmers like yours truly. A lot will lose their farms. That's what.

Even the big farmers aren't protected. Say they raise their pounds and the company don't want it. They got plenty coming in from overseas. Drive the price down to nothing. Tobacco is done in this state and nothing to replace it. Hemp rope made us heroes back in the old war, but now it's illegal. Politicians all running scared.

My farm is like most Kentucky farms, hills and ridges and only a few acres of arable land. You've got to make every one count. If an acre of corn brings two hundred dollars in a good year, an acre of tobacco four thousand, what would you do?

I can't believe I've lived to eighty. Probably because I never took up smoking. I tried it out, but could never establish the habit. Hands always too busy.

Eighty. Around here, a man outliving his wife is unusual, but I guess losing a child is harder on a mother. I'm real proud of the one I've got left, even though she married a Taulbee. Eighty and not bad looking. I could probably get a date if I had the heart.

Everything has got automated in the last fifty years, everything but tobacco. Planting, weed chopping, cutting, hanging, stripping; it's all still done purely by hand. The way the

Indians in Virginia showed Captain Smith. The way I showed my daughters.

I clasp eleven cured leaves in one hand, wrap the twelfth leaf around the top, tie it to make a hand of tobacco, red gold and smelling sweet, the first of the season.

I trade it with my neighbor; I peddle it at auction; I enter it in the county fair.

Will Colter

IF YOU LOOKED outside your window at five o'clock from most anywhere in Bourbon County, you could see wild geese advancing in a wavering V toward Gray's Pond, following Will Colter's van. When Will got there, he would pull up into the marshy spot at the edge of the pond and park just as the geese swooped down and struck up their chatter. He'd unlock the back doors of the van and reach in for the burlap bag he kept filled for them, clucking as he scattered corn and sweet feed in the high brackish grass.

"Now, now," he'd say, "It's not like any of you'uns is fallin' off an ounce." Then he'd throw the corn up high so that some would fly up to catch it in midair like gulls. "Chase it, Sadie," he'd shout. "Fat's how I like you." When he finished feeding, he'd stand with his hips jutting forward and his back a little hunched from bending over all day and stroke his bushy black mustache.

The remaining contents of Will Colter's van represented

his livelihood: three toolboxes of different sizes and degrees of use. One for plumbing, one for carpentry and one for yard work. A magnetic sign stuck to the side of his van read:

WILL COLTER

REPAIR, MAINTENANCE AND LANDSCAPING

REASONABLE. NO JOB TOO SMALL

WRITE P.O. BOX 37, PARIS, KENTUCKY 40361

Will didn't have a telephone. Everyone local knew him so they either chanced into him in town or drove down to the old Fitzpatrick place where he lived and left a note on his door. No one thought much about disturbing him because, since he'd quit drinking and since Frances left, he stayed pretty much to himself. They knew the work would be done the next day.

Will did such fine work he was considered practically an artist. His plumbing never leaked and his yard work was immaculate; he always trimmed and swept the sidewalks. Part of his secret was knowing so much about everything. He knew the kind of grass to sow for certain results, the right tool for certain jobs, and partly it was that he took his time.

He was partial to woodworking, always going to the extra fine grade sandpaper which most people don't take the trouble to use. Then he rubbed linseed and lemon oil into the wood instead of just floating a coat of varnish on it. "Wood is supposed to breathe," he'd explain to his customers, holding their gaze an extra moment. "You should let it." Will's eyes were a rich blue and so pronounced you could see the gold arrows that shot through them. They disarmed people.

After that, customers regarded their new banister, or shelf, or tongue-in-groove planking as if it possessed some special charm. They'd say to their neighbors, lightly touching their lemon-scented bookshelves, "Well, as you know, wood breathes."

Folks were glad to have Will back in town, and especially pleased to have a dependable odd jobs man around, glad that he'd settled down and stopped shaming his mother with his drinking and philandering. They'd understood it, had seen many young men go through that phase, most ending up marrying too young, some of them dying on these blind, hilly roads. They'd kept their peace, just hoping he'd live through it.

Will's drinking started after high school, when he moved up to his daddy's cabin on the dark side of Hawk's Nest Mountain. Most of Eastern Kentucky was dry, so there was good business in moonshine which is what Will's daddy did.

"Ain't nobody's 'shine like mine," he'd say. Shirley Colter was an enormously fat man who wore bib overalls and house shoes year round. "Nope. Not for seven counties. Quality of the mash. Quality of the still. Real copper tubing. Quality, son. No substitute for that." He'd lean over and spit tobacco juice into a tin can he kept by his side.

Will's parents had gotten divorced so long ago that he never thought of them as ever having been together—his mother with her flour-white skin, thin, arched eyebrows and half-glasses on a chain, his father with his week-old salt-and-pepper stubble, tufts of white hair sprouting out of his ears. He couldn't imagine that they'd ever inhabited the same house. Will lived with his mother during the school year and was sent to his daddy's place for a month each summer. He helped his daddy brew corn whiskey, black beer which he bottled in horehound-colored glass to keep the light out, homemade wine out of everything from peaches to dandelions, and brandy so strong it rose in vapors.

When Shirley spent weekends in Louisville with his friends on a corn or hops run, Will threw parties. He danced with the loud women his friends brought over from Paintsville and Germantown, drinking his daddy's hooch and flirting his head off. He'd always invite everyone to spend the night.

"Now where you all gettin' off to?" he'd say when they made to leave. He'd be smiling, stroking his new downy, mustache. "No need to be chompin' at the bit. Everything's gonna be there when you get back." He'd smile and blink both his eyes as if when he opened them they'd have a new perspective on the situation. "Right where you left it."

Everyone liked Will because he was generous with his liquor and laughter and because he made even big-footed Germantown boys feel like dancing. Late into the night he would fix "Dirty Willy" pancakes and scrambled eggs. In the mornings he'd step over them like a cat, as if he were shocked to find that he had company. He'd be so surly everyone would gather their things and leave. But when Shirley left town again, Will would manage to round up a gang for another party.

The town at the foot of Hawk's Nest Mountain was named Whitesburg. During the hazy, timeless summers, Will learned the trades that he would eventually rely on by following Shirley's buddies to their yard work or plumbing jobs. Evenings, he'd help with his daddy, who made fine oak and walnut cabinets or, when he got a request, maple and cherry rockers. The summer after Will graduated from Bourbon County High, he moved a lot of his things into Shirley's cabin. He considering locating there permanently until Shirley came home unexpectedly from Louisville and happened on one of his famous parties.

One afternoon in early August, Will rolled into Paris, hung over, and hauling a Nester girl from up in Frenchburg. Four of the girl's bottom teeth were missing, which gave her kind of a bulldog look even without her fullback's shoulders. Will stood in his mother's hall. "Me and Daddy fell out," he said. "I was wondering if me and Rhonda could trouble you for a place to stay?"

The next morning Will rose for an early breakfast with his mother. She watched him shuffle red-eyed and bedraggled to the coffeepot.

"I'll not turn you away," she said to Will's back.

He ceased pouring.

"You've got a week to find a job. A month to find a place." She picked up her Burpee's catalogue, read for a moment, then added, "And don't marry that Nester girl. At least your father did have better taste."

A month later, Will moved into a duplex in the housing projects with Rhonda. Sometimes their arguments spilled out into the street so that the neighbors, drawing back their curtains an inch or two, could watch, excited and dismayed. One Monday Will awakened late with a headache, a memory, and an echo. The memory was that both he and Rhonda had been fired from their jobs in the jean factory for habitual tardiness the Friday before. The echo in his head sounded familiar though he did not recognize it at the time as his father's: It takes two to argue.

He walked into the living room where Rhonda had passed out on the couch. He woke her and with a voice both gentle and resigned, said, "Let's quit this." Rhonda sat up immediately awake though her eyes were swollen from having cried half the night. She bit her lower lip and nodded. That afternoon Will put Rhonda's suitcase in his mother's Buick, which he'd borrowed for the occasion and drove her back to Frenchburg. She went peaceably but with her mouth dropped open in surprise, her teeth like lonely stalagmites.

He stopped by Shirley's cabin on the way home. The old man was splitting wood on the hickory stump perched on the hillside. Will picked up a splitting maul and worked with him in silence for almost an hour. They grunted as the wood cracked. Will's boots ground into the fallen persimmons, strewn about like dissolving opals, stirring up a sweet, acrid scent.

When they finished, Shirley eased himself onto the stump. He contemplated his house shoes, then Will. "You're looking peaked, son," he said, dipping into his snuff pouch. He tucked a wad of mint Timberwolf under his upper lip. "But maybe the Lord's done give you a second chance."

When Will drove back to Paris in the slow fire of a red dusk, his mind seemed to make a quarter turn and he decided, without forming any particular thought, to become someone he liked better than the man he now was. The old crowd dropped off, not interested in making the two-hour drive to

Paris just to watch Will pace around stroking his mustache in total silence. He still allowed himself the soft oblivion of corn liquor on holidays and occasional Saturday nights. But even then, he was no longer rowdy. He sat alone on the stoop with the Blue Tick dog he'd gotten after Rhonda left. He sat, his legs elegantly crossed, stroking his dog in an attitude of waiting and, after his cousin Oscar's wedding, thinking of Frances Banta.

Normally, Will wouldn't have gone to the wedding. Period. But it was important to his mother that the groom's side of the church be filled with a respectable number of people. When the congregation sang, Will was struck by a rich alto voice across the aisle from him. He managed to catch a glimpse of her when they rose again to sing: a tall dark-skinned woman in an old-fashioned pastel suit. She wore wire-rimmed glasses, which Will thought strange on a woman who couldn't be much past thirty. At the reception, he managed to stand next to her. He rocked back and forth on his heels, stroking his mustache, smiling and shaking hands with everyone. After the guests arrived and things settled down some, Will asked if he couldn't get her some punch.

"That sounds good," she said, with the same thrilling alto. She met his gaze with curiosity. That afternoon Will learned, from meeting the rest of the family, that Frances was the only dark woman in among several ruddy blondes. She looked Indian or maybe Mexican. According to Aunt Jerky, no one in the family knew about her real father, although everyone realized that she was not Charles Banta's daughter, since Charles was a Swede.

The duplex was beginning to oppress Will. After some

futile searching, his Aunt Jerky told him that Beulah May Fitzpatrick had finally died and that her sons were keeping the farm but trying to rent the old house.

The house was really a large cottage, where Beulah May had continued to live after her husband, Harley Coleman, died. Her sons tried to persuade her to move in with one of them, but Beulah May refused. "I'm fine," she'd said, tightening the corners of her apron to secure her snow peas. She was on her way back from the garden and in no mood for her sons' silliness. She glared from beneath her bonnet. "And I don't need you boys here underfoot. If I need something, I'll let you know."

Beulah May lived far enough into the next spring to see her tulips bloom. That early April morning, she drank her strong, grainy coffee and watched them for a long time while they trumpeted their colors in a red and purple circle around the weeping cherry tree. They found her in her bed, the covers pulled up and lying perfectly straight.

Her sons auctioned off her belongings and distributed her canned tomatoes, pickle relish and ground-cherry jam to their families. There was so much of it that they left some jars on the shelves and when Will came to see about renting the place, they told him he was welcome to it. The place had gotten run down in the past few years, so they made a list of repairs that needed to be done. Will agreed to do them instead of rent, which was a good arrangement since the brothers wanted to raise tobacco and tend the farm without worrying with the house, and Will was completely broke by then. They showed Will the enormous turnip patch Beulah May had planted on the far side of the garden.

"She remembered the Depression like it was yesterday," one of them said, regarding the patch. "She didn't ever want to run out again."

Soon the cottage was completely enclosed in green. Will took his showers under the rusted gutter pipe and went about repairing the house, fixing the eaves and replacing the window sills with wood he found in the barn. He soldered pieces of pipe together to fix the plumbing, which had burst in Beulah May's absence. During those months he made use of the canned goods and turnips: turnips with butter, turnips with relish, fried turnips with polk and wild onions. Turnips and eggs.

Will's mother got him a few odd jobs in town so that soon he had the money to buy real gutter pipe, stove pipe, a chain saw, and to make a down payment on a van. He bought tools as he went, depending on what each job required. He seemed content, poking around town, stroking his long, black mustache, with that self-possessed air he'd had even as a child. When Will called on the older folks around town, they noticed that his manner had not changed from childhood. In elementary school, his teachers were always surprised such a diffident child took such care with his handwriting or his science projects. His quick hands were expert and almost graceful, except for the exaggerated joints.

As an adult, his hands were long and knotty. "Philosopher's hands," Aunt Jerky called them. And the rest of his body matched: high knobs of cheek bones, bent and angular back and legs, close-cropped curly brown hair. Will matched the shadowy and unpredictable landscape, the foothills and knobs, that rose around him, making the skyline jagged, mirroring the silent, inscrutable man he had become.

Passersby who saw Will hiking on the ridges of the old Coleman farm like Beulah May did were reminded of her and were comforted. They watched him in silhouette, already bent, as if with age, with his muddy slew of dogs. Most everybody appreciated his handiwork, tolerating his undue consideration for animals, even when his pack ran their cattle and horses. He lived peaceably, tending his dogs and birds, taking in strays that happened up to his house.

There was Blue Tick, Phaedra Two-Eagles, Cassandra Moonbeam—a scraggly excuse for a dog—and a red dog named Pippa, that Will found with his paw caught in a fox trap up in Pippa Passes. It ran on three legs offering the mangled paw gratefully to anyone it met.

The farm's beauty was not lost on Will. He kept a kind of journal of his impressions and sent these pages off as letters to Frances, who seemed daily to be drifting closer to the center of his thoughts. He'd pause on the ridge, playing the scene of their meeting over in his mind. He ambled, smoking, blowing smoke rings in perfect O's, thinking of her voice, the clear blue gaze so like his own. After a month of letters, Frances sent him an invitation to dinner with her family over in Olive Hill. Will whispered the news to his Aunt Jerky, so the whole town knew by Friday.

Folks had been wondering when Will was going to find someone besides those dogs to keep him company. The only girls he'd dated seriously since high school were the Lanier twins, first Darla then Drema. He liked them both but finally was not able to choose between them. That was all, except the Nester girl with that mouth like somebody had bowled a split.

The man Frances shared her Sunday dinner with seemed to her rough-cut, overly shy. When she said good-bye to him at the gate, she wasn't sure she wanted to ask him back. But the man in the letters saw things in finer detail, seemed to breathe a more rarefied air.

In his letters, which increased both in length and frequency, he described the day moons over Gray's Pond, the fiery sunsets. He drew sketches of the dogs and stray cats and their exploits with dialogue in balloons above their heads to amuse her. He chronicled the wildflowers as they bloomed: Jack in the Pulpit, Lady Slippers, Virginia Bluebells. These entries were an inner record, which he offered to her. When he visited, Frances was obliged to keep the conversation going, sometimes carrying on foolishly about things she didn't really care about, nervously filling in space. Yet when she opened the thin, blue envelopes with their smooth, black script (Frances thought his handwriting resembled musical notation), she found a different man. She savored each week's letter until the next one arrived. She hoped Will was the man who might eventually protect her by understanding her.

Will's business peaked during the summer with yard work and carpentry and then diminished and steadied in the autumn. Most every Saturday night, he and Frances could be found on the porch swing in front of the Bantas' house. Will kept the chains oiled to keep them from squeaking and thus interrupting Frances' voice, which flowed through him like melancholy music.

Will brought half a sugar-cured ham to Thanksgiving dinner at the Bantas. At the table, he cut thin, translucent slices, arranging them with soft, clinking noises on a flowered china platter.

Charles and Alma Banta both thought that Will's prospects were dubious at best. But they also realized that their old money was actually threadbare. Nor was Frances, thirty-five and their only unmarried daughter, the youngest. They encouraged her to ride this particular current. Frances was talented as a painter of family emblems, coats-of-arms and the frontispieces of fireplaces, but that provided only enough for her share of groceries with a little left over for paints. Her talent was inherited, no doubt, from her real mother, who Aunt Jerky discovered out after some party-line research, was an Indian woman Charles' brother had gotten pregnant and was unwilling to claim. Through a series of events, Frances had ended up living in Charles and Alma's house where she learned that asking questions about her parents only caused the taciturn nature of her aunt and uncle to deepen. As a teenager, she looked around the table at her fair-skinned family and decided the issue didn't matter anymore. This capacity for restraint gave Frances an air that many mistook for coolness of character.

At the request of the bride and groom, neither family attended the wedding. Will's mother provided the diamond solitaire that had belonged to her grandmother and the Bantas sent several items of furniture to Paris, which Will tried to place at their best advantage inside the old cottage.

January 22nd was a sweet day for Will. There had been a

new snow the night before, cold and bright, like confectioner's sugar. He had busied himself since early that morning making little paths back and forth to the woodpile to get the stove rocking hot and to be certain of a three-day supply on the porch. He had also worn paths to the dog pen he'd finished just the day before, knowing Frances would not hold with dogs in the house. He'd broken the ice out of the dogs' water dishes and treated them with fat scraps and bones from the butcher. "Get back, Cassie, Pippa. Get back, now." Will said, locking the gate, "I'll fetch you this evening." The dogs whined and minced in the snow, their hot breath smoking into the frigid air. That morning he made several trips to the hay barn and the well. As he retraced his steps, the little paths took on the color and texture of brown sugar.

At eleven-thirty Will closed his front door, puffed his chest out a little and patted it, a gesture which might have seemed more fitting to a man in his seventies. He set out into the clear day in black wool slacks, a white shirt, a thin red tie and a short jacket of soft leather, a Christmas gift from his mother.

He drove slowly in the warming truck to the bus station, not wanting to arrive too early. On the way, he passed a gang of boys throwing a football back and forth. They yelped and barked, beating each other down into the snow, shrieking with pleasure. When he stopped at the light by the courthouse park, he saw a large woman lying on her back in the snow, making a snow angel, demonstrating for her child, who only stared at her. Finally, she put the child back on his sled and trudged on.

Will arrived early anyway. At twelve-fifteen, two people disembarked into a cloud of diesel fuel. The first was a well-fed college girl carrying a burgundy gym bag, then Frances, frail in a patterned dress and overcoat both too thin for the day. She smiled, approaching Will.

"Well, here you are," Will said, placing a hand on each of her shoulders as if they were two knobs of satin glass.

"Here I am," Frances said.

The house was still warm when they returned after stopping by Justice Simpson's for the twenty-minute ceremony. The judge's wife acted as witness. When he helped her with her coat, Will noticed for the first time the outline of her shoulders, her breasts.

In some ways, winter is best for romance. Some come down with cabin fever, but those in the spell of new love have a secret smile when they look out into a blowing, snowy morning. That is the way it was with Will and Frances. Flakes fell and fell, mesmerizing them, giving them a sense that the house itself floated solitary into the air. They clung to each other in tenderness against the cold, and retreated together from their former desolation with passion and relief.

"Dear Fanny," he whispered when they made love in the iron bed under layers of quilts. *Fanny*, the name he had used in letters.

Whether it was the thaw that turned Will outward toward the hills again or if it was his spirit, somehow spent, that turned inward, Frances couldn't tell. But by spring, Will's manner had changed. This change was not acute, but his touch seemed impersonal, his eyes distanced, his words even more sparse. She noticed this after lovemaking, when they saw each other at the end of the day. He would meet her gaze for a moment, close his eyes briefly, then open them as if to dismiss her.

A litter of pups from Pippa increased the dog crew by five, and the whole crew seemed to grow edgy. They weren't satisfied in their pens and they barked at everything. "Think we got enough dogs yet?" Frances asked Will one evening as they sat watching the new sycamore burn and pop with quick blue flames in the grate. He glanced up at her and smiled, as if closing a door.

One morning, Will brought in a black kitten with four white paws and a white blaze on its forehead, one eye swollen shut. Will thought it was just an infection of the inner eyelid, but when the wound resisted healing, Will took it to Doc Patton, who told him the kitten had a tumor. The operation set their finances back so far they couldn't pay rent. "Them Colemans ain't going hungry," Will said, swabbing out the kitten's eye. "This one needs tending."

Frances watched Will all bent up, hunched over the little kitten, stroking it delicately. She knelt down and stroked one of its paws. The kitten retracted, curling in upon itself. Frances sighed and went on with preparing supper.

One afternoon in early summer, Frances mowed the yard, blowing the grass inward so she could rake it. "You're mowing it twice," he said, reversing the direction of the mower, "You mow it, then you roll back over it. You're mowing it twice." She pushed on, noticing the edge in his voice, the slight flare of repugnance in his nostrils. Suddenly, she hit a snake and the mower choked and died. Will leaped down into the grass. "A copperhead," he said, touching the skin of the still writhing creature whose body had been completely severed. "You ought to be able to tell when one is near," he said, trying to keep his voice even. "They smell like cucumbers."

By mid-summer, he was late for supper nearly every night.

"Where you been, Will?" Frances would ask, turning the pork chops.

"Had to work late," he'd answer, getting his tools out to clean them at his workbench in the pantry. "Days are longer now." Then he might rise and step over to kiss her. By August, Will was coming in so late that Frances just saved supper for him in the oven.

He'd eat around midnight, big meals, letting the blood pool in his stomach, dragging him into sleep. The rare times he was home, he watched her intently until she became so self-conscious that she made mistakes with whatever she was doing. Then he'd flare his nostrils as if he'd expected it.

"Can we talk about this, Will?" Frances said, one afternoon when he'd come home early. She'd been cutting lard into flour to make pie crust. She wiped her hands on her apron and turned to him.

"Talk about what?" Will said, fishing his whetstone out of the drawer and lining his knives up on the work table. He raised both his eyebrows as though waiting.

She turned back to her crust. "I thought that after a while you'd warm up a little, you know, that we'd be closer."

Will stopped the blade on the upstroke and held it for a moment. He looked at her. Then he dipped it in water and smiled. "Now Frances, I think we get pretty close."

"It's like opening up to a cold wind," Frances said and Will winced as though she'd slapped him.

That night they lay without sleep in the old iron bed while Frances wept. Will turned to pat her shoulder, but he did not take her in his arms. After a while her tears began to suffocate her, so she turned on the ruby-glass lamp by the bed. She saw her husband there, caged in shadows, his eyes brimful with terror.

In October, Frances and Will dug new potatoes. Stopping for a moment, she watched him slide the fork into the ground in the perfect way he did everything, making it seem easy. His inscrutability, like an impenetrable gloss, shut Frances out. She was in his world, but not of it. And she hadn't a world of her own. He had taken her in when she had few prospects and she was grateful for that. But it wasn't enough.

"Good crop," Will said, leaning on his shovel. "Maybe we can take some into town and stick them for a nickel."

Frances didn't answer him. Finally, Will looked up.

"Will," she said. "I've got to go."

For a moment their eyes met in recognition, then Will seemed to take a step back.

"Well, I wish you wouldn't," he said.

Frances wiped her face with her red bandanna and returned it to her pocket. She watched him brush soil from the potatoes until they were nearly clean, then place them in netted sacks for drying.

On their last day, Frances made sweet rolls for breakfast. Will stayed in the living room watching prize fighting. Frances set his dish next to him, glanced at the TV, then Will, then left the room. She was moving back to Olive Hill. Her mother had helped her find a place with a family who would give her room and board in exchange for tending their grandfather. They'd even contracted her to paint the Griffin family coat-of-arms. With Christmas coming up, Frances could probably get several orders.

"Alma will be here soon," she said. "I mean, if you want to talk before I go."

Will gazed into the screen.

In the bedroom, Frances latched her suitcase. She heard Will switching channels. She heard cartoons, then laughter. When Alma came, Will carried her suitcase to the car. Frances looked at him, her mouth the little white line it had become sewn into the past year.

"I'm sorry," Will said. "But I wouldn't offer you something I couldn't live up to, something counterfeit."

Every afternoon around a quarter to five, folks in Bourbon County notice the wild geese following Will's Colter's van. Of course, what else were people doing at five o'clock of an evening, driving home from their shift at Bluegrass Industries, home flouring chicken to fry, or riding around in jacked-up cars? What could they be doing that would prevent them from just glancing out into the iron-gray that combines with the gold of a winter sunset to see a flock of wild geese flying overhead. It seems the whole town stops quiet, holding its breath, aware of that moment at the same time each day. Not that wild geese following a man is anything mystical, just unexpected, like most things Will did.

Will had gotten a new dog, a miniature sheep dog, if there

was such a thing. He'd named it Andromeda Outpost, "Andy." The dog went everywhere with him, even to Gray's pond because he didn't chase the geese.

"You'll get your fill," Will said, casting sweet feed into the grass. "I can see none of you'uns is going hungry. But that's all right. I like you solid."

Will returned the tin cup to the burlap bag and checked the contents: enough feed for a good week even with the cold weather. The sleek birds circled on the lake, leaving cold gray swirls in their wake. In the unnatural stillness of the day, he stood beside the van, a small, finely made man, handsome and slim in his khaki pants, comfortable as though cold weather never bothered him. He knew how to dress against it: long underwear, caps with ear flaps and sheepskin gloves, wool socks and lined, lace-up boots.

In the quiet of the bluing day, he leaned against his van, smoking, perhaps thinking of the woman who had come to him in short days like these and who stayed while they lengthened, whose unintelligible pain caused her to leave before the next solstice. Maybe his memory was like a spice of grief. Or perhaps, gazing out into clear evenings, blowing smoke rings into the orange and indigo sundown sky, he thought of nothing. Perhaps he was only living through the day, tending the creatures he dared to tend, moving in their silent company, through a season where even noon has a hint of midnight, those blue days of winter, so short they don't seem real.

Chenille

CUDDLE UP TO ME, Anne Evans said, and Dory did. Every night she stayed with Anne, she waited for those words. It was Anne Evans' senior year and she'd just been voted Best-Looking Girl in her class. Straight brown hair, dark slanted eyes, tempting fluted lips. Every cute guy in school had asked her out.

Dory might have gotten elected "Best Baby Fat" or "Most Likely to Trip Over Her Own Shadow" if her eighth-grade class had made categories. She spent the night with Anne Evans at least three times a week, sometimes coming over after Anne Evans' dates.

They would dress in cotton pajamas and slip under the chenille bedspreads and hug each other tight. Dory listened while Anne Evans relived out loud everything that had happened on the date.

"Ritchie Lykins said, 'Anne Evans, if I couldn't go all the way with you for five years, I would still marry you.'" Anne

Evans kissed the boys in idling cars in her parents' driveway. Kissed. That was all. She was a good girl and she instructed Dory to be a good girl, too.

She taught Dory lots of things, like how to roll toilet paper around your hair to sleep after you'd been to the beauty parlor, how to use a tampon without killing yourself and the importance of wearing tunics.

"Some of us are born high-waisted," she said, her hands on her hips. "Not our fault, but no need to advertise it."

Anne Evans' mother cooked the old country way. Heart attack food, Dory's mother called it. Her daddy worked graveyard shift at the typewriter factory. He slept all day in the house with the curtains drawn. Everyone had to tiptoe around Anne Evans' house in the biscuit-scented dark to keep from waking him. Anne Evans broke up with Ritchie for touching one of her breasts at the drive-in and two days later she was dating Dan Chancellor, the basketball team's all-time high scorer.

Anne Evans always fell asleep before Dory did, clutching Dory's hand to her belly as they spooned in the Hollywood bed. Dory played the details of Anne Evans' dates over and over in her mind till she was dizzy. Anne Evans always smelled good, Ivory soap with a touch of boy's cologne. English Leather or Jade East, depending on the boy.

Dory tried to locate Anne Evans' teenaged face in the soft contours of the middle-aged woman sitting across from her at Applebee's. She was Mrs. Dan Chancellor now; they'd celebrated their twenty-fifth anniversary in June.

"Thanks for your sweet letter," Anne Evans said. "I showed it to my kids." She stirred sugar into her iced tea with a straw.

"I meant it all," Dory said. The chicken wings in front of her appeared to have been candied. "You took good care of me back then." Dory wanted to know Anne remembered those nights under the chenille bedspread.

"How's your Mom?" Dory asked, dipping a stalk of celery in blue cheese.

Anne Evans picked up one of Dory's chicken wings, broke it open and had a bite. "Mom's been sick," Anne Evans said. She glanced around at the hanging stained-glass lamps, the retro sixties décor, then settled her gaze directly on Dory. The same dark, slanting eyes, full of candor. Her beauty flashed out at Dory again. "You probably don't know this, but the doctors sewed Mama's privates up my senior year in high school," Anne said. "She never discussed it, but she wouldn't let Daddy touch her after that. One time, she caught him stepping out with one of those factory women and that was it. Kicked him out of the house. Never forgave him." Anne finished the chicken wing and delicately pressed a napkin to her lips. "Do you have kids?"

"Kittens," Dory said. "Cats and dogs. I'm a veterinarian."

"Pick them up and hold them," Anne Evans said. "I read somewhere that animals can die if they don't get that." Anne drew iced tea up through her straw. "My parents never touched me. Not one hug. Not one *I love you.* I make a point of telling my kids I love them at least once a day."

Anne Evans and Dory talked till the lunch-shift waiters had all gone home and the happy-hour customers began to drift into the bar. They laughed about all the silly things they'd done back then, tearing fruit loops off the backs of boys' shirts and dancing the jitterbug in the gym every morning before home-room. Anne Evans reminded Dory about the time she'd had to teach Anne Evans "The Jerk" and "The Locomotion" the day before the prom.

"I was basically a nerd," Anne Evans said.

But Dory hadn't remembered it that way at all.

Kentucky Bluegrass

I HAD A FRIEND in high school in Kentucky whose name was Jimmy Clay Bledsoe. His parents, Brock and Elizabeth Bledsoe, were both teachers at the high school. The Bledsoes arrived at school every day at seven-thirty and left together at four o'clock. They seemed to be very content and in love with each other, with a son who was quite brilliant.

Jimmy Clay was a model-train expert, and every year at the Science Fair he set up his trains with tunnels and crossings and miniature landscapes around the entire gymnasium.

Jimmy Clay was the school's fat boy. He didn't mature sexually during high school, never had any facial hair and his voice was high. There is a picture of him with some other boys who'd been selected to attend an academic competition in another town. Jimmy Clay is bent forward to get into the car, with five boys lined up behind him. Jimmy Clay, the fat boy, laughed at through eternity in the high school annual.

When he went to college he was singled out for cruel

practical jokes, smoke bombs and caps of nitroglycerin. After college, he just came on back home.

I had a few dates with Jimmy Clay. He called me one day when I was living back in Vance on my farm. He came in a little Honda car to get me, the first one I'd ever seen. He had a lot of facial hair by then, a full beard, with little tufts high on his cheeks like a werewolf and his voice was low and muted, like the sound of the lake ice splintering as it thawed in spring. He had taken up exercise and dieting, so he wasn't fat anymore.

Jimmy Clay was meticulous with his car, taking off his shoes inside so he could operate its tiny pedals. He lay down paper mats on the floor to protect the carpet. On our dates, we went to car dealers; Jimmy Clay was looking for the perfect diesel-powered sports car. Or we would go to the airport and watch the runway lights, and I'd listen as he talked reverently about planes.

One of Jimmy Clay's hobbies was birds. He kept a clipped Toucan on the screened-in front porch where Brock and Elizabeth rocked back and forth on the glider to fan themselves.

Jimmy Clay kept two blue macaws in his room. They were so loud, I had to wear a soundproof headset just to be in the same room with them. He said he liked macaws because they mated for life. That was one of Jimmy Clay's goals, to be like his parents, to be happily married, mated for life. But he'd been too strange in high school to even get a date, and was too contentious with me. We fought about everything, like the fact that I didn't shave my legs, which Jimmy Clay said was not feminine.

I had another friend in high school, named Emily, who was in Girl Scouts with me. For years, sixteen of us saved up our money from bake sales and then we all went to Mexico. Emily was an innocent sort of person. While we were all drinking nips of tequila and crème de menthe in the taxis so our chaperones wouldn't see, Emily walked the hot, crowded streets of Mexico City gazing up at the vast pink buildings. She was tall, with dark skin and dark eyes that were so open I always wanted to close them with my fingertips. She always seemed younger than the rest of us.

Emily was on a date at the drive-in her senior year when a blood clot passed through her brain. In a small town, when these things happen, stories are invented. One rumor was that Emily was drinking and on drugs; another that she was taking birth control pills. Now in 1968, no high school girl was taking birth control pills in the entire state of Kentucky. If you did have sex, you didn't admit it, and most of us really didn't. Nobody knew why this had happened, only that she was not right after that and was put in the Midway Hospital and has been there ever since.

A couple of years ago, I was visiting a friend who'd had a baby and when I walked down to the hospital's nursery, Emily was there too, in her wheelchair, looking in at the babies. She looked the same, as dark and innocent as she'd been at seventeen. I guessed she looked that way because she hadn't had the same job strains or sun exposure or relationship problems as the rest of us.

"Emily!" I said, and she looked up and smiled and even said hello, but I could see she didn't know me.

So a friend of mine told me the latest news: Jimmy Clay and Emily had gotten together. They go out on dates. Jimmy Clay picks Emily up at the hospital and drives her to the airport, to his new plane, a Piper Cub. They take off down the runway and climb into the sky and survey the farms and patchwork of fields below.

Kentucky has rolling hills of timothy and clover and something called bluegrass. When you are looking down from a plane, you can see how the wind ruffles though the tall, strong grass, like a hand. In the shadows are shades of blue. And Emily loves to look down at it.

Then they go to Jimmy Clay's house where he still lives with his mother. Brock died a few years back and Mrs. Bledsoe is retired. She sits in her easy chair and reads boxes of books that she buys at auctions: mysteries, classics, Harlequin romances. When she finishes, if she hasn't been to another auction, she starts over.

In this house, four generations of Bledsoes have lived. There are so many stacks of things on either side over your head that you have to negotiate a narrow path from room to room. The house is clean, but filled with layer after layer, every magazine and university bulletin, every piece of train track that Jimmy Clay ever collected.

Jimmy Clay comes in the front door so he can push Emily through in her chair. And in the afternoon he and Emily sleep on the couch in the sun, there in the living room, while his mother reads in the den. These are the two things Emily likes best, she likes to sleep and she likes to fly and she's happy that she has someone to take her out of the hospital and who cares for her. Jimmy Clay is happy because he finally has someone he can devote himself to, always. He has found his beautiful girl.

Bull of the Woods

MAYBE SHE SHOULD NOT have been her father's oldest son, being a girl and all. Maybe we should not have gone to her parents' house those weekends and ordered Gino's pizzas, large. That pizza was the specialty of her hometown, a watery town, where the Big Sandy River rushed by opaque, clay-red in spring, and where her father had his houseboat: *The Bull of the Woods.*

Maybe we should not have stayed out all those nights on *The Bull of the Woods,* because the men came at noon on Saturday, toting coolers jam-full with sirloin steaks and Little Kings Cream Ale. There's always enough beer and wine in a dry county if your daddy's the county attorney. Here they came, all the bulls: Uncle Mac and Uncle AJ, laughing and breaking beer bottles over each other's heads, where their hair grew back in white-blond patches; her boyfriend, Benny.

"Got a lot invested in this," Benny would say, grabbing his belly, tanned as a Hershey bar.

Their profusion was so sexy. They made everything seem easy, made me almost believe there would always be plenty. "Eat as much as you want, drink as much as you want, drink until we have to carry you home in a Dixie cup."

Pour us in the boat's narrow bunk, where we traced finger-tips across lips, sought breasts through Oxford cloth blouses, kissed deep like sun-warmed chocolate. Maybe we should not have taken so many chances, ventured so far out if we were not going to venture all the way across the river.

There is always a woman who can't stay, who crawls back through the woods.

"Dive," Benny and Uncle Mac said to me, at sixteen, dizzy on Cream Ale in the sun. I stood, my feet planted wide for balance on the top deck. They'd been diving all day, jack-knives and cannon balls, the boat pitched when they pushed off the ledge, then righted itself.

"Dive," they said.

And I did. A swan dive. I crouched and my thighs gathered power. I believed I could be like them, could charge with the force of bulls, could take what I wanted. My feet pushed off, and time slowed, as though their gaze held me for an extra moment, arced in the air, while they toasted with full bottles ... before Benny found you out, before he proved that he was stronger, before we knew how fast the river runs at flood stage.

There's always a woman who can't stay, always a woman calling, let her tell you her story, about the girl descending down and down, her hair flows behind her like a flame, extinguished by the warm waiting river, let her tell you her story. Pick up the phone years later in the middle of the night, the ring that wakes you like a gunshot. Listen to her story, about the girl who dives down and down into the fast red waters of the Big Sandy.

Sín Verqüenza

A COKEHEAD AND A JUNKIE are two different things. With junk you hit up and just drop out. You feel very benevolent, but all you can do is sit there trembling and nauseated, your eyes slamming shut. With cocaine you are fascinated by your own mind, you feel smart and interesting and full of energy. Your life is suddenly ideal. Then the high is tainted by the craving for more, and you rev and rev till you climb the fucking walls. I do coke but I'm not in the gutter, you understand. I'm a worker. I save all my money past rent and food for my Friday night dates with the snowman.

Both my jobs are seasonal. Factory work in the summers, winters I cook. Right now I'm at the Del Monte plant in Stockton, California, July through September. Peaches. Tomatoes. The factory where I work houses three levels under one rippled tin roof. From the outside, it's just a square concrete building about the size of a city block with two stacks on both sides pouring out steam round the clock. This building is joined to another one just like it by a tin bridge where the cans ride back and forth. That building is prep, where the peels are melted off with lye, rinsed, pitted and halved. Both buildings are windowless. Once you shut the doors, it's another world.

My building is the actual canning plant, the floors are concrete with colored stripes leading to different departments. No walls inside, just sections for each job and layers of people working the machines, monitoring each step or working the line. When I applied for the job, I expected a lot of fancy, incomprehensible machines. But everything was simple, primitive even, like something a tinkering kid might throw together for a science project.

It gets so humid that around two A.M. when it is cool enough outside, the steam condenses on the tin roof and rains down onto the night shift; which is Black and Hispanic. The swing shift is Asian. The day shift, white. On night shift, I was the smallest, whitest person in the plant. At first they called me "Small Change," but because I whistled so much they thought I liked the job, and changed my name to "Easy Money." There's the smell of steamed tomatoes and spice. The people who add spice wear respirators to keep them from sneezing to death when the salt and pepper and dehydrated onion dust is churned up by the mixers.

We screw earplugs in against the noise of cans clattering in their wire chutes, the huff of the seamers, the rumble of the graders shaking the fruit forward into the flumes, the hum of the belts, the people trying to yell over top of all that. Some people wear whistles.

After three seasons at Del Monte's I've been switched from

graveyard shift to days. I could have been transferred to can watcher or filler supervisor but I like clean-up crew, so I stuck with that.

I work with hoses three inches around and a steam gun that melts people inside their banana suits. The bosses didn't think a female could do this job, especially not one five feet even and weighing in at a hundred and one.

"Half-pint female like you, I don't know," the big boss said, sizing me up and down. He looked to be an old fullback gone to seed. He shook his head, shrugged his shoulders: what the hell.

First few weeks I admit I was strictly faking it. Even now it isn't easy. The sweat pours from beginning to end of my shift, with me holding to my limit doing double time. I've picked up five pounds and dropped an inch in pant size. I'm solid.

You wouldn't believe how much Freestone peach crud can accumulate on a vat in a matter of minutes. Clean-up crew works on adrenaline. We're everywhere at once, doing things no one else will do. I do things even the rest of clean-up crew shuns, jumping out on ledges that are covered with peach slime and swinging down to get at the backs of the vats. If I go into work too tired to face it, I toot a few lines and cover the whole factory. I read the Peruvian Indians used cocaine when they were traveling for days, working hard without food. I imagine myself an Indian scaling mountains and hightailing it across the desert while I shovel hard down among the flumes.

Pipes of different colors run along the ceiling, deep red for hot water, white for cold water, key-lime green for the structural beams. I spend a lot of my time up there on the catwalks doing the high-risk hopping around.

"Hey, monkey," the foreman, Fred, calls to me. "Watch your step." This other guy, Paulie, looks up all concerned. This Paulie has a special interest in my not breaking my neck because he has a jones for other parts of me. I can't take him seriously, though, because of his ducktail, which shows out from underneath his hard hat.

I start at the top and work my way down, till I'm actually underneath the bottom line workers and all I can see are rows of white rubber boots. I scrub the flumes where the sorters have pitched extra-select halves, slicers or peach parts so ragged they get sent to concentrate. Tomato flumes are worse. If you don't get every seed they lodge and sprout.

If I said the factory was primitive, I did not mean it wasn't beautiful. The tomatoes run the chutes like churning rubies. The peaches come bunching down like fragrant, overripe flowers. And for all the sweat and sloppiness of the job, the result is precision: long white belts with perfect peach halves, tins moving in procession after being stamp-sealed, bathed and twirled into their label. You can spot the grunts in the blue hard hats, the officials in white, and the safety men in yellow. If you handle product, you wear white aprons, white boots and white rubber gloves. The order of these workings give me a secret pleasure.

The factory itself is cruel to the body. Sorters, the people who work the line, stand on metal or concrete. They shift back and forth on their feet, trying to get comfortable. Steam burns are common for the seamers. One woman got her arm hung at the end of the belt and was wedged there with her bones breaking because the foreman had refused to tell the line workers where the on-off switch was. That's one reason I like my particular job. I figure if I can keep moving, I'll avoid some of the pain.

The accidents are usually the prettiest part, like when the tanks overflow and peach or strawberry chiffon poofs out. The factory produces six million gallons of water a day from the fruit. One day a pipe burst and couldn't be fixed until the entire factory floor was half a foot deep. When the afternoon shift left, I just lay on the catwalk while the white boots, doubled by the water, filed out. The whole factory reflected up like the ocean casting back a monstrous, machine-age sky.

This guy Paulie doesn't even know my name. Before he was hired, a salesman came around at lunchtime peddling stick-on letters for our hard hats. Instead of putting *Amelia*, I bought silver letters that spelled MONS V. None of the guys had a clue what that meant and I was mysterious with them when they asked. So this guy Paulie comes on crew and says, "Hi, Mons. I'm new on the crew and glad to meet you." Right away, it's a big joke, everyone on crew calls me Mons like they forgot my real name.

I'm suspicious of Paulie because he's probably gotten the idea from girls along the way that he's some kind of hunk. Plus maybe he's already heard about Sully. That boy had been after me for two seasons with me pretending not to notice. But this season, the clean-up crew got together for a little party at the Two Keys, and I let him drive me home. I figured why not. We didn't even go in my apartment, just romped around in his van, working it all out in half an hour. He kept repeating the whole time how I'd been driving him crazy for two years. I stuck to walking home after that. But I know how men talk.

Maybe you're wondering where someone like me learned about the Mons V, the Mound of Venus. I'm not ignorant. I read books. My family had me educated at fancy preparatory high schools. Not that you can't be educated and ignorant, too. My parents are proof of that. I try not to put on airs. I grew up thinking if I tried everything once, I could be realistic about my choices.

I don't know where I got that idea. It certainly wasn't from my family. They seemed to just have one idea that got trumpeted my entire life and it wasn't even a good idea to begin with. Get ahead. But they disagree about how. Same stiff dinners, same exact fights on Saturday night. My mother drew more and more inside, her head sinking into her shoulders like a turtle, her shoulders rolling forward. My father did the opposite, his chest popped out more and more, and his back began to sway, like a bad horse.

Coming to California from New York City was about as far as I could get from them in the continental United States. I've got my own plans. Big plans, too. When I was little, we spent a year in Spain and my father took my brother and me to bullfights on Saturday. To me, they weren't cruel. Those bulls were descended from ancient fighting bulls and their only aim was to kill. If the matador faces him head on, arches his body over the bull's horns and buries his sword in its heart, it's an inspiration. At twenty-five, I still fantasize about being a matador. I wear a pink brocade suit, skin-tight. I never flinch.

Today is Friday and I'm feeling good. I've got everything planned. It takes me forty minutes to wedge the steam gun into a safe place to keep it from snaking all over the factory at one hundred fifty pounds per square inch. I mount the belt, remove a stainless steel cap almost as tall as I am. The circular, twenty-four-inch blades glitter as I steam them clean. I am the only person on crew who will do this job. I like being hot and I like the idea that I am preventing others from possible harm. I finish just as the shift whistle sounds. I twist the steam off and remove the hard, heavy gloves. I unscrew my earplugs. The belt winds down and I can hear the workers. One big sigh.

On my way to the lockers I feel a hand on my shoulder. I know it's Paulie before I turn around.

"So, Mons, some of us are going for beers. Wanna come?"

I smile. Just one, I say. And I mean it. I don't want to blur my high.

So it's four of us sitting in a booth at the Two Keys over a pitcher of brown beer, suddenly the *in thing*. Fred, Sully, Paulie and myself. It's shop talk for about an hour as if we can't help it. Union steward doesn't seem like he's working for us. Cooker number nine's gonna kill somebody someday soon. On and on, like exorcising demons.

Paulie keeps my beer at the brim. His hair is slick and shiny, blue-black like handsome hoods in Sunday morning cartoons. His chest pumps out beneath his T-shirt like he just had it inflated. Shirt too small, tight. Good muscles. Nice house. Just not sure I like who's inside it. Funny how men try to look as big as they can, women as small.

"So what kind of name is Mons?" Paulie says. "Sounds French."

The guys elbow each other slightly.

Paulie's eyes are dark, his eyebrows darker. His eyes are so deep set and watchful, the whole room flows into them. His mouth has a definite shape, the top lip with two pink peaks.

"That's not my name," I say. I'm stepping off a cliff saying this to the boys. But so what. They might as well have a little education about the thing they spend half their time talking about. "It's Latin, actually. Short for 'Mons Veneris.' My name's Amelia."

The guys drink beer. Somebody is winning big on the pinball machine. Paulie still stares.

"It's the woman's part," I say.

"Oh! Pussy!" Sully says, like he's struck by God's lightning bolt.

"You mean you're advertising your cunt on a hard hat?" Freddie says.

Paulie's hand draws up slightly.

"I have a mons veneris, a Mound of Venus." I give Paulie a look. Back off. I can take care of myself. "I don't guess you've ever been to an art gallery, have you, Fred? That's about the only place that treats female nudes with any reverence." I nestle back into the corner of the booth. "Maybe you ought to check one out sometime before you die."

"I guess you'd rather I say bosom and not tits?" Freddie says. His tight lips smile a white smile.

Sully's eyes look past us toward the wall of pinball machines. Red and orange lights flash in his eyes. Bells clang and ding.

"I'd rather you didn't say either one," I said.

"How about penis and not dick?" Freddie says.

"How did we get on this subject?" Sully says, banging his mug on the table.

"I get it," Paulie says. He is diving into my eyes. He smiles. His teeth are very white. "You're something else."

I'm smiling, too. But I want to get away.

My mind shifts to last weekend. I was arranging my works on the bureau: a liqueur glass with distilled water, cotton, rubbing alcohol, a sterilized spoon on a clean saucer, the syringe, spare points, an X-Acto knife and the white envelope. The phone rang. My sister. She's having trouble with her husband.

"I have to go," I said. "I'm in the middle of washing the dishes."

"I need to talk to you, Amelia," she said. "I'm afraid of him."

"Okay," I said. "Listen. I'll call you tomorrow."

That was bad, I think, pushing my beer glass to the center of the table. It occurs to me to call her tonight, but then my mind busies up with excitement.

"I'm gone," I say to the guys and lay down money for my beer on the glossy wooden table.

"So soon?" Fred says.

"Later," I say.

"Monday, seven A.M.," Sully says.

I'm halfway down the block when Paulie catches up with me.

"Can I walk with you?" he says. I keep on walking. "Wanna go for a bite to eat?"

"Got to get home," I say. "I have some calls I have to make."

He wonders can he call me later.

"Maybe tomorrow," I tell him and give him the right phone number on a book of matches.

"Are you okay?" he says.

I tell him I'm fine but I'm ready to scream. Thinking about getting high has made me urgent.

"Are you sure?" Paulie says. He has that look of concern that used to always haul me in back before I discovered what fakes people were.

At home I run my bath deep and hot. I strip my clothes off and stuff them in the hamper. I lay out my works. I am so excited I begin to shake a little. Thinking about getting high always makes my bowels move.

Then I'm ready for the bath. I put one foot into the water, too hot, but I let my foot find the bottom and turn red. I am very still. Stirring the water makes the heat unbearable. I wait for the first foot to adjust then shift my weight to it and put the other one in. I sink down, slowly, hardly moving until I am sitting, then I lean back wrapped in hot silk. My mind is calm. It's all right, I tell myself. You still have your life.

Being a junkie is not like being on cocaine. A junkie needs to get high just to feel normal. Cocaine always makes you high. If you're just obsessed with it and it hasn't taken over your life, it always makes you high. And it always makes you feel awful.

The first few times I shot cocaine, Tim did it for me, of course. After the first rush, I was serene, sensual, excited but not agitated. The first few times I let Tim do it. We'd been dating for months, but the first time I knew about it was when he asked me to come into his upstairs bedroom after a party. He worked at a veterinary clinic so he always had clean needles.

My first time, the crystals were totally pure, pharmaceutical cocaine.

"Just like Sherlock Holmes used in between cases," he said, tying himself off. "In those days it was legal, like it should be. Hospitals used it for anesthetic." His next door neighbor banged a metal lid on a trash can. "Good quality, not laced with anything." His eyes went hard with concentration.

I dropped my arm and pumped my wrist as few times. I've got good veins so I didn't need the tourniquet. The needle pricked in with no pain. As soon as the drug entered my bloodstream, a clean, medicinal taste suffused my mouth and nose. Tim had trouble getting the needle out of my arm. "I should have done you first," he said. "That was stupid."

My heart raced as if it would burst, a giant egg of terror broke and spread inside my chest; this was followed by a sensation of hilarity, which reached through my fear and yanked me to the other side. Tim jerked at the needle, then pressed a cotton swab with alcohol on the puncture. I crooked my arm to hold it and lay back in bed. An overwhelming, *in-love* type orgasm rushed through my body in a long ecstatic wave.

Tim lay down beside me, moaning a little. For the first time since junior high church choir, I began to sing. After a few minutes, Tim joined in and we sang everything from old Donovan songs to show tunes. I appreciated everything: the sheets, the neighbor's door slamming. Every word he said or I said was suddenly charming and magical. Tim had tin foil fastened to his windows to reflect the damning Southern California heat, which made the room dark and still. We pushed them open and listened to the palmetto leaves slice deliciously through the breeze.

It seemed the world flowed in and filled our veins. It was the first time in my life that I did not fear joy, and joy filled me.

When we started to come down, Tim shot us up again. The second time was good, but not as good as the first. After a few times, I realized maybe it would never be as good as the first, though I kept hoping. When Tim did himself, he would draw his own blood back into the syringe after the first hit to rinse the syringe out and shoot it in again. I swore to myself I would never stoop to that, but by the second or third session, I was milking it worse than he. We kind of stood guard those first few months to say, "That's enough, hon," and draw the needle out.

After a while, I became more secretive. I shot up while Tim was not there and more and more I wanted to do it alone. Tim was a social guy, he'd have people over and they'd party. I stayed in his room, which embarrassed him, I think. Finally, Tim found another girlfriend and moved in with her. Though I told myself that broke my heart, nothing was as important as my nights alone. He left his old maroon-and-gold school jacket, The Juggernauts, with a varsity speech letter sewn on the back and a crate of brand new needles. That was last year.

Now I must be alone. At first I did yoga while high, I felt strong in my mind, never scattered, entertained by my own thoughts. I like the whole process. Needles appeal to me.

I get out of the tub, oil my skin and slip into my satin robe.

Tonight I have half a gram. Two good shots, and two scrap shots.

I worked like an animal all week, and only did a few lines. I worked for this. I deserve this. Last November, I temped in a secretarial pool and quit coke. I went out dancing with some office workers, perched on a bar stool and waited to be asked to dance by some man who assumed he could grope you all night if you said yes. I had lost a whole world, and I didn't like the new one.

This is my world. Where I earn my dollars through honest sweat, where I can see what I accomplish. On weekends I explore my mind. I am looking for that thing that I will create. Everybody has to create and when I do, I will rock this world. I will have pushed the limits, seen just what kind of distortions of reality I can return from. I'll bring back my offering. Something new, something that has never before been said.

I find the triangle of paper in the bottom of my drawer. I won't have to go to the dealer again tonight. I am already shaking and my throat feels tight, right at the back, swallowing, very slow in my movements, quite careful in my ritual. I am right there. I lift some of the cocaine out of the paper with an X-Acto knife, which I have wiped with rubbing alcohol, as I have done the spoon. I am most careful taking the cap off the needle, which I do now, using the cap to stir water into the cocaine. Too slow, and you can bend the needle getting the cap off; too fast, maybe you stab yourself. I always err on the side of slow. Anyway, the cap is off, I draw 25 milliliters of water into the syringe and then squirt it into the spoon.

I stir the powder and water with the red cap until the powder is dissolved. Then I make a tiny ball of cotton, roll it between my fingers and drop it into the center of the spoon. This filters any large impurities. We learn from the ones who died this way. Junkie lore.

Now I swab the inside of my elbow with alcohol, make a

fist, loosen, make a fist, loosen, until my veins stand up. I am very excited. I place the needle point into the cotton, draw the solution into the syringe. I flick the side to get the air up to the top, then push it out with the plunger. It takes a lot of air to interrupt the heart enough to kill, but air bubbles hurt.

I fuss a little bit with the angle of the syringe in my hand before I am ready to hit the vein. I place the tip of the needle, slanted-angle up, at my vein and then with a tiny thrust, I am in. Just so slightly I pull back on the plunger with my thumb and the silk parachute of my blood seeps into the syringe and billows. This is good. It means I am definitely in.

Slowly, I depress the plunger. As soon as I am in the vein, I can taste cocaine in my mouth and in my nose, not quite a scent, the clean, longed-for flavor that means I am about to get high. I am getting high, my mouth drops open, I am riveted on the needle in my arm, careful not to move and lose the vein. I check it, still in. I push the last little bit in fast and I can barely keep going, but I do, pulling back on the plunger, filling it with blood and then faster in, feeling a huge rush, just at the edge of control.

I want it. I want to get away. I've never been answered and this answers me. I take out the needle and lie back, pressing cotton into the crook of my arm. I have it. I want it. I have it.

I ease the needle out, put the tip into the liqueur glass and fill it again. I lay it down carefully, even this high I know how desperately I will want that cocaine-tainted water later. It is all I can do to get to the bed and lie back. My breathing is very conscious, shallow, through my mouth. Every pore of my body is laden with pleasure and there is a buzzing in my head, almost audible. When Tim and I mainlined during the day in summer, the buzz of the locusts resonated with ours. We'd shove open the tin-foiled windows and laugh.

The phone rings. I answer it without getting up.

"Do you know what is happening with your sister?"

"No," I say.

"It's Mark. He's beat her up again."

I can hear my mother's Chihuahua yipping. Many times I have imagined shooting that dog. A gunshot, then sudden, blissful silence.

"She's over here," my mother continues. "This time I don't know. I think he's hurt her really bad."

The dog stops yapping for a merciful moment.

"Amelia. Are you there?"

"Yeah, Mom. I'm listening," I say. "I'm sorry. But I was on my way to work."

"I thought you changed shifts," my mother says.

I tell her the clean-up crew is being called in for overtime.

"I'll call you as soon as I get home," I say. My eyes watch the water-filled syringe as though it might move.

"You told your sister you'd call her yesterday."

"I know, but then this came up. I'll call."

"Don't forget," she says. Here is my chance to get off the phone quickly.

"I promise."

I jerk the phone wire out of the wall and reach for the syringe, greedily shooting it in a stream into my mouth—that pleasant bitter numbness.

Knowing how soon it will end starts to ruin the sensation.

I'd lost two, maybe three minutes of a fifteen-minute high on the phone.

When we went to the bullfights I cheered as loud as anyone. It never entered my mind that cheering the event was unkind, that primitive bloody spectacle in the sun. I knew that in the early days before armor, the horse always died. The bull can raise the entire horse and rider and cast them over his back. The picador must move around the bull and dig his lance into the giant neck muscle, weakening it, so that the bull finally lowers his head. Otherwise, it is impossible for the matador to reach the heart.

The men chant and yell if they do not like the picador. The tourists join in afterward, in imitation. I never pitied the bull because the bull himself is without mercy. He is the Minotaur waiting in the labyrinth, a partner to young, acrobatic slaves in a dance to entertain the king, an actor in a play with fellow creatures he would not hesitate to kill.

I make my second shot. This is a large hit, and for the first few moments I wonder if this is too much. I am out of control again; all I can do is lie down. I winnow down to the core of my mind, to the tenderness and hurt. Here I find my sister, very small and full of hope. I see Dixie Green, my best friend from second grade. My most frequent memory of her is the day she led me back to the room from the playground where I was lost. I see the boy who ran in circles around the schoolyard drain yelling, "Neal Jackson's dead! Neal Jackson's dead!" Neal Jackson, who made his sevens with a little hook, who fell into the neighbor's well. All the girls had lined up so he could make that special seven on their papers. Neal Jackson.

If the matador is brave, he allows himself brushes with the bull, stepping aside with a flourish from behind his tiny cape. At last, the matador points his *espada* toward the bull and advances. He arches directly over the bull's horns and plunges the *espada* into the heart. If he has been skillful and brave, the bull dies immediately.

Women throw hats, everyone throws flowers, the lame throw crutches hoping to be healed. Once, I saw a live pheasant thrown into the ring. And instead of running squawking, it calmly displayed itself as though proud it was about to be sacrificed to such a brave man.

But if the picador has picked too much and the bull is weak, it is not honorable. If the matador stabs the bull slightly to the side the *espada* lodges in his lung. He does not die immediately, but stands drunkenly, head down, bleeding from the nose and mouth.

The crowd is furious. "Sín verqüenza!" they shout. "Sín verqüenza!" You have no shame, no shame.

If the bull is also brave, if he does not charge the matador when his back is turned, then he is also celebrated. It is impossible to know when a cowardly bull will charge.

For me, the blood running down the side of the bull was not blood but just more brightness, like the colored banners on the *banderillas* and the matador's suit of lights.

Knowing the bull is not indifferent, I was awestruck by the beauty of the matador's passes, thrilled by the efficiency of his kill, his mastery of a huge animal who wanted to kill him.

I am never the woman with the hat or the man with the pheasant. I am the matador himself. I am the dancer. I dance for loves buried in my chest, for my dreams of love.

The high becomes tainted by the anxiety of losing it, of wanting more and not having it, of it being over. The fear subsides into regret, because that edge of disaster is where I want to be, nothing intrudes on sensation there.

In ten minutes, maybe fifteen, I can make my way back to the spoon for my scrap shot. I have left the first water in the syringe from the liqueur glass. I am hurried, knowing the shot will be a good one. I rinse the paper off into the spoon, less careful now to have only 25 milliliters of liquid; the less liquid, the less chance for anything to go wrong.

I don't know what, really, air in the syringe, losing the vein, or heart valve infection, cotton in the syringe—I've done that, extremely painful, possibly dangerous. This time I don't get the vein the first time and when I do, it infiltrates, and I lose it.

I start over, over and over again, until the high has degenerated into obsession and anxiety. I spend half an hour poking holes in my arm, till I get a good scrap shot, but I am not as high as the first shot and I am immediately possessed by a desire for more. I put water in the syringe and boot it over and over, jabbing at the vein, all the other veins, seeing air in the syringe, then blood, then the blood clotting, starting over with a spoonful of blood, only slightly bitter with cocaine. Removing the clot and shooting the blood, barely bitter into my mouth, missing, squirting blood on my face, blood against the wall. By then, I loathe myself.

And at times I have wanted to die, though when I came close, I forced myself to stay awake through the horrible ringing in my head, knowing I was too high. My room spun in a vortex which filled with yellow light as I became smaller and smaller.

Tonight, I lie in bed with my clothes on because I am too uptight to take them off. I may have to go out to a dealer later. I don't want to see my body.

I spend a couple of hours planning how I will go to the bank and take out the rest of my money and get cocaine with it and come home and shoot it all, never run out. I lie on my right side, then my left, turning over and over until finally, at dawn, I fall asleep.

I wake to the sound of pounding at the door. I sit up in the loose sheet. My arm is sore, both arms, punctured like a pin cushion. I am sick at heart. I put up my works and wash the blood from my face.

I see Paulie through the high square window. He looks relieved, sweaty.

"I've been calling you all night," he says when I open the door a few inches. He rubs his arms as if he is cold, but it couldn't be that cold, could it?

I wonder where this Paulie gets off worrying about me, but I keep that thought to myself. I open the door, allow him past me. I offer him tea, while he fidgets on my only chair. His manners are gallant and self-conscious. I am earthbound, mechanical. I pour the tea into the cup, wondering whether to wait till it steeps, or just hand it to him. I consider the quickest way of getting him out of my apartment. I can't bear to think about what I was doing only a few hours ago.

The teacup jiggles in the saucer in Paulie's lap. Growing up, I never wanted to sleep with boys. But I did it because I thought it meant I was tough, not a sissy.

I pull off my jeans and climb into bed. I leave on my long-sleeved shirt.

Paulie's face turns scarlet. "You think guys are creeps, don't you?" he says.

"Aren't they?" I say.

He is speaking but I don't hear him. The noise is in my ears again. I close my eyes waiting for it to pass. I am repentant, prayerful. I will never do this again.

Paulie sets his cup on the floor and sits on the edge of my bed. "Come here," he says.

"What do you want, Paulie?" I say.

"I want you to put your clothes on," he says.

We lie on top of the sheets, if he notices the spurts of blood he doesn't say anything. But it's dark in here. The scent coming off Paulie is musky and minty and sweet. A boy smell. I don't want him. I thought I could always come back to this kind of desire, but now it seems a parody of my real desire.

I used to believe that everything would turn out for the best, that there was a benevolent presence behind things. If something appeared evil or brutal, it was a kind of joke, like my parents pretending that they had forgotten my birthday.

I liked the bullfights. I didn't associate the blood rolling down the side of the bull with suffering, with life flowing out. I didn't connect the buckling knees or the cheering crowd with death. I didn't know that the bull had stood in a darkened pen without food and water for three days then released before a crowd thirsty to see life forced from him, a debilitated and tortured animal that in the end cannot even hold up his head.

When the heartbeat leaves the bull, there is a corresponding blood heat in the heart of the crowd, a sensation of power, near riot, a delusion that death can be defeated; this, through the courteous and formal man bowing in the center of the ring. The bull is bred for this moment.

I say to myself that I will not do this again, but I know I will. Like wrapping the rest of the cocaine, cocaine I promised myself I would not shoot, in an envelope, in another envelope, inscribed with the name of someone I think I love, someone who represents goodness. Of course, I tore into both envelopes, did the cocaine. Nothing mattered as much as that.

I feel depraved. I seem to float slightly above my bed while Paulie holds on to me. If my body stays this way, some lost part, a part that helped me care whether or not my sister was beaten by her husband, maybe might drift back and I will become myself again. Paulie's body has relaxed and his breathing is lengthened. Knowing he is asleep, I look at him. His lips droop a little, his good muscles go soft. I see for a moment that he means no harm.

Then I turn back to my thoughts. Like I said, I'm not stupid. I read the experts. Like the theory about this button in your brain that gets pushed whenever someone says I love you, or that's a good job you did. I read that supposedly cocaine pushes that button over and over and over, so that when someone does tell you these good things, that button has been over-pushed so much it doesn't matter to you. But there's the bad button too, when I lose control with my scrap shots. I have the idea that there's more coke in the rinse and that more will make me happy. So I dig and dig into my arms for nothing, not caring what I'm putting in myself, not caring what I'm doing to my body. And remorse paralyzes, keeps me from doing any of those things I plan. Somebody should make a theory about that.

Sometimes on Sundays, I go to the University of the Pacific to check out books. I find a bench in the grassy park and watch the students coming in and out of the dorms. I imagine what it would be like to be in one place like that for four years, to have all the decisions made, classes in place, a precise goal. Maybe I'll walk Paulie over there, read him a book in the grass. For a moment I breathe in the peace of that idea.

I examine this Paulie, his hair so slick it glows even in the half light. I tell myself all he wants is a little ass, a little Mons V. When he wakes up, I'll get him out of here and track my dealer down. The day, as they say, is young. I don't need this guy or anyone else and that's honestly a relief. I'd rather be alone with my bath and my works fucking my arm with a needle. Coke is something I can predict. Something no one can take away from me. Something that is mine.

Some days, I come back from lunch a few minutes early and lie on the top catwalk, gazing at the colored pipes. I like it up there where it's barren; I like the transitory, machine quality. I feel like I've always been there. I hear the cans being pulled down by the sensing switches that know when the level is low. Before the lid is stamped, the edge is so sharp it can slice your finger in two. They're lined up on a reverse roller coaster, the fruit and syrup dumped in, the lid stamped on. Once a cricket jumped off Fred's shoulder into the can, dead center on top of the fruit. Before he could say anything, the lid came down and the can was whisked away. We always tried to picture the chump who got those peaches. I savor those moments before the whistle, listening to the cans rattling by. I can distinguish them by their size, from pings to clunks, five separate notes.

Pretty People

I ALWAYS THROW A PARTY on my birthday, which is in July. I do whatever I want and absorb all the affection that wafts my way. No other day but that. Too much happiness, I get tense.

Down South, the air can go chartreuse with the excitement of ozone, a tornado like black granite plowing a path straight to my house. In Boston, in July, you might be freezing cold or practically melting on a tar roof, a fiery wind blowing city fragments in your eyes.

I write on the party invitation, "Rain or Shine."

One year, two of my friends came as me. One wore a ribbed undershirt and fatigues, axle grease slathered across her arms. She carried a red plastic Uzi, leapt into the yard full of people quietly discussing movies, and pumped the gun, soaking the crowd with long streams of water.

"HURT FEELINGS!!!" she caterwauled.

The other me stuffed her bra with socks and let people sign her jacket with a laundry marker, penning supposed quotes from me, like, "We have to talk" and, "Pretty people can't be trusted." They both wore Dolly Parton wigs.

In the picture of the three of us, it's clear I am not really a buxom blonde with overwhelming needs. Not compared to them.

I'm always arguing with someone in my mind, honing my logic with their anticipated remarks. I never say, Oh yes, I see your point. There's also a person in my mind I'm trying to please, to whom I offer my best black irises. I unfurl for them and they never step on my petals, crushing them to veiny pulps. They never do.

I invited a soon-to-be-ex-girlfriend to my party, a cop who'd had a hit-and-run accident she didn't remember because she was in an alcoholic blackout. When the squad car showed up at her house, she aimed her own gun at her head.

They didn't fire her, but took her gun away and put her on some kind of horse pill. I should have known that first night with all the dogs in cages, the parrots and love birds flying free, dive-bombing me as I went to the toilet. She talked in her sleep about "going down to the station" and always seemed restless. Her ad had read: "Extremely attractive. Ethnic. Seeks engaging conversation."

She was first to arrive at this year's party and I sent her down to the backyard with the CD player and a bag of balloons to fill with air. Between chopping eggs for potato salad and soaking chicken breasts in marinade, I looked out the window to check on her. Instead of party music, I had accidentally left a disc in the player with sounds designed to alter your brain waves and ease you to sleep. The rhythmic sea-like pulse drifted into my third-floor window and there she was, lovely girl, curled on the lawn in party clothes in the brightest nest of balloons.

Your Cheatin' Heart

THIS IS WHAT I KNOW about people: they are secretive and can't help it. They feel a need to hold exclusive access to their innermost soul. But I know this, too: if you are patient and attentive, people reveal themselves to you at every gesture and turn.

My girlfriend, Scottie, is an aficionado of music. Her conversational style is singing lyrics at you with her fist of a microphone anchored in the air one inch from her mouth. She thinks of herself as a spirit cowboy, a laid-back hedonist whom everyone loves, and she is right. Scottie is one of those charming, pretty women with glowing, resilient skin who is at her best in groups.

Her proclivity for waste, excess and the vagaries of privilege is canceled by her thorough lack of guilt and the energy to accelerate past all the chaos in her TT Roadster, Mephisto sandals and linen slacks from Bloomie's. She possesses a silver aura.

These are trying times, when you can't turn on the television in Gotham City without having George W. Bush or the Verizon Corporation make false promises—and this is what I know about my girlfriend: Song lyrics are the key to her subconscious.

Not the obvious jump from passing a hound dog on the street to a curled-lip Elvis impersonation, but a more complex expression, arising from silent musing until her mind seizes upon a phrase which she then repeats for the next several hours or days. It is important to know all the lyrics to her songs, because the kernel of truth lies beyond the chosen phrase.

After our first blushing months of romance, my girlfriend shifted into a personality very like a tri-mode cell phone. She picks up three signals: one, the outburst where her pretty face becomes bellicose, a deep ravine crimps the space between her eyes and she resembles a carved mask, an angry God whose words ricochet among her trio of peeves—cat hair, money and my alleged lack of attention to her; the second mode is the captivating four-year-old who uses wit and tears to charm her way through any eventuality; and third, the perseverater of lyric.

"Do you always have to sing pop songs?" I once asked her. "Can't you just talk to me like a regular person?"

"Not pop songs," she replied, with her now-familiar contemptuous snarl. "Alternative rock."

I listened helplessly as her lyrics transmogrified from lush Nat King Cole and U2 ballads, *but we'll carry each other, carry each other—one love,* to the defiant, misogynist brayings of the Rolling Stones and Robert Plant, *cuz I'm free to do what I want, any old time.*

"I'll never cheat on you," she told me from the very start.

I took this to be a bad sign, an even worse one when she stopped saying it.

Last week, we were cruising to Provincetown in her convertible, when she gazed at me and sang with all her big, pink heart *When tears come down like falling rain ...*

I followed the lyrics to the end, the molasses and vinegar of that old Hank Williams song, always one of my favorites.

Desconsuelo

HE ALWAYS MOVED at the same pace, working smoothly as if lifting the bags of mulch, digging, bending to the plants, required no effort. A fine rain fell. His paths lay raked and groomed, a corrugation of soil and sand, the trellises newly black, without rust, the grassy courtyard even and bright. And then the roses. She ventured out for them. Her habit these past months—were they only months?—was to live indoors, ordering groceries. Not often, not many: crackers, potted meat, a few oranges, all spiced with the lemon pepper her son Jonathan had liked, putting it on everything, even his cantaloupe in the morning.

Not that she was trying to die, no, that was what she must not do. Because if there was hope—and hope was the wafer that fed her—then it lay in living. But, if she got diabetes, or was pitched from a bridge due to a sudden gust of wind, well ... she could not be blamed.

She entered the garden, her eyes avoiding the roses. Her

small, tight body was erratic, as if on some other errand. She checked for others but there was only the gardener. Good. She lit a cigarette and sat down on the edge of the courtyard, her feet on the path. As she smoked, she put the ashes in her palm.

Her mother once told her that close and cloudy days were the best time to chase the scent of the roses. It was all right.

"She is beautiful, yes?" The gardener gazed at the statue behind her, a reclining white marble nude draped over two steps, her hair camouflaging her face.

"But, faceless," Julia answered.

"Yes," the gardener said. His face reminded Julia of a rodent, a handsome rodent with small narrow eyes, reddened skin and nearly white hair.

"What's she called?" she asked.

"*Desconsuelo,*" he answered, looking at the statue another moment, then moved on and began clipping the overblown roses, placing them in his green wheelbarrow.

Julia studied the sculpture. The woman was well carved, especially her hands. One held two fingers of the other. A delicate touch, each hand supporting the other, liberating the whole figure. She knew desconsuelo meant disconsolate in Spanish, but why not a feminine title for her, the grieving woman, the brokenhearted woman. Maybe it meant just sorrow. She placed the cigarette stub in the bottom of her coat pocket and left the garden.

Julia's new apartment was nearby. When she moved there she had been impressed by the building's ornate white facade. She thought it was made of marble, but a few days later she noticed white paint peeling from the wooden cornices. Today, three young girls had set out a formal tea party on a crate by Julia's steps. They rearranged themselves so she could pass. "Good afternoon," one said.

"Hello, honey," Julia said, not looking at their faces as she hurried past them.

At the top of the steps she turned and descended again. From her billfold, she drew three dollar bills, folded them and handed them to the one who had spoken. "Your party needs a cream pie. Go down to Tim's Bakery and get yourselves one."

"No ma'am," the smallest said, "my mommy says ..."

"Now, hush," Julia said. "It's all right. Go on."

"Thank you," she said and accepted the money.

Julia climbed again the single flight of stairs to her apartment on the north side of the building. She wanted to sleep. But she must not. She must save sleep for night. She didn't want to risk insomnia. If she could only fight through these first minutes. The apartment was silent. But still better than having a television or radio. She had no telephone, no mirrors. The only sounds were made by Julia, or Vera, Jonathan's cat, whom she had brought along at the insistence of Jake, her ex-husband. Sometimes she could hear people talking in other apartments. Her own apartment was so silent she couldn't help but listen. She enjoyed hearing them, especially the arguments. She felt pleasure in their anger, their resistance to each other. When she heard them, she felt gratitude.

Julia had come to this place to be alone with Jonathan. She had been forced to leave her farm. At least for a while. No one had understood Jonathan's death, not even Jake. No one seemed to understand what had happened, nor did they think she should be alone. They were frightened. They hadn't understood. They had only talked and talked and she couldn't concentrate. They used the wrong words even though she told them the right ones—the event, in the other time, the resting place.

Vera made a noise. Not a meow exactly, more like a tiny scream, and Julia went to the kitchen to feed her. As she opened the can, she was shocked to see her own eyes reflected in its lid. Big eyes, like Jonathan's. Everyone said so. They had lived through each other's eyes. She could get back to him. She knew it. She had only to get away from the interference.

She thought about the resting place on that final morning. She was sure she had seen him there, pointing to the flowers then to the same color in the sky. He had shown her. She understood.

Julia watched Vera eat her supper. She wondered why the cat always dragged the bite she wanted to the middle of the floor before she ate it. She picked the lid of the can up and looked at her eyes again. They were too big, really, and always red-rimmed as though from crying. Her niece had said that her eyes looked so big that they hurt and Julia had smiled and had hugged her. She liked to hug Clare, to feel her small round body, so dense and solid, to touch her bright, cool skin. But that was in the other time.

Now her eyes were empty except for dreaming. She wanted to sleep. She would fall away, yielding to its luxury, the promise, entering a world lit with the faint light of her urgency, rushing to meet her child.

The next day the roses were bright, shocking; but Julia was

more at ease. The tall, deep hedge enclosed and silenced the garden. Julia bent to a blossom called *Angel Face* and inhaled a hint of sweetness. She stopped by the marble nude. The figure seemed to be at peace today. Julia tried to read the statue for the story of her sadness, but the woman seemed to be resting. The only sign of pain was a hidden face. She wanted to see the face, to find her cold white eyes.

"I tell painters to come at different times of day to paint her," the gardener said from behind.

Julia tensed, though his tone was not expectant.

"I tell them to come in the morning while there is still mist, and in the afternoon, to see the shadows changing. She has different ... moods."

They both regarded the nude woman. It occurred to Julia to feel embarrassed, but she wasn't. She especially liked her long, white marble hair.

"She seems peaceful," she said.

"She is lucky," he said. "The rest of us have to get on with it. She is simply *Desconsuelo.*

"My son likes roses," Julia said.

"Oh. You have a son?" the gardener asked.

"Yes, but he's not here." Julia moved away from him and sat on a stone bench to smoke a cigarette. How she wished they had visited here in the other time. Jonathan loved flowers, and still loved them she was sure. He called roses by their names: *Brandy, Peace, Lady X.*

"You are Lady X," Jonathan had once told her, cupping a bud with his hand and sniffing it. Jonathan and the flower were the same height.

That's when her flowers were on the rise. California poppies were folding down their flat petals, like upturned palms, with brush strokes of paint, orange on yellow. The blossoms seemed to float in air, nestled among the jagged lace of frail blue stems.

After he turned six, he wanted to help her with everything. They were sweating hard, digging, arranging the flat stones, their lungs full of the cloying scent of the magnolia.

Julia hadn't liked Lady X before her son said that. She thought the color unnatural, too pale purple with a bitter edge. But now she could see its rare beauty. Today, when she left the garden, she moved close to the lavender flower, and touched it, lightly, as one might touch the face of a lover after a long absence. Without belief.

Now Julia felt the thinness of her life, like a photograph, fixed at the moment of the event. She understood the pieces and occurrences of her life in the other time. She understood what he meant when he spoke of his cousin Clare.

"I love Clare," he said one day when they were driving.

Jonathan had his bare feet on the dash of the their custom-painted mauve Chevy Luv pickup. "I didn't know that," she said.

"Of course," he said. "How could anyone not love her?"

It was true. How could anyone not love her?

Another time, an artist had given Julia a very good price on a painting of a woman in the countryside. The woman was admiring an iris she'd pulled up by its roots.

Jonathan said the painting was evil. That's when Julia saw the rapacity of the woman, destroying the plant which she exalted; she saw also the obscured image of the artist in the background. She gave the painting to a visitor who came to buy corn.

If her life was now a photograph, it was lived in its negative. She prayed for death. She prayed that the cancers of others would enter her body so that they might live and she might be with Jonathan. Suicide meant she would never see him.

Before she left her farm, she had talked to everyone who had known him. She asked them to remember special things he had said. She wrote phrases down on pieces of cardboard. She memorized them. She would live by these. She would purify herself.

Julia sat smoking, although she knew Jonathan wouldn't approve. She was thinking of the night Jake stood over him, drooling into his face, pressing him down on the bed in nothing but his underwear, his wrists trapped in Jake's grip. Over, what was it? Yes, hadn't put up his toys the way Jake told him to. She remembered the nearly empty bottle of Old Overholt on the dresser among the dusty pictures: her mother, a school picture, her father, smiling his handsome, critical smile, perfect in his naval suit.

"Can't you remember ANYTHING?" Jake shouted, shaking him and gripping his wrists tighter, pressing him farther into the bed. "You're a stupid boy and you can't remember what's important."

Jonathan hadn't answered him. He only stared in amazement at his father. She knew his look. It must have been her own expression every night at the supper table, when her own father found a reason for ridicule. She remembered always crying through dinner. They had to clean their plates. But it was never the chores, and it wasn't bad manners either. She was plain, not full of charisma and good looks like her father. And she wasn't going to be.

Toys weren't the problem, either. The problem was the nail polish on Jonathan's fingers. The problem was the lipstick.

Jake asked her in a scornful tone if she was worried. Well, no, she wasn't worried. What was the difference between that and the way he looked when he got into the blackberries, or the day they ate all the popsicles on the way home from the store. The dots of color with which he adorned himself, his slender body of light, were merely signs of the innocence of a five-year-old. No, she wasn't worried; not about that.

Now, sitting in her apartment, with Vera on the window-sill looking out into the city, Julia smiled at the memory. She remembered Jonathan's wordlessness as he carried Jake's possessions to the storm door with the glass kicked out and threw them out one by one, his pipe and fancy pipe tobacco, his sketchbook, his pottery, which clanked but didn't break, his empty wallet, and finally his empty bottle, which broke with a muffled sound, shattering into a fine snow of glass in the creases of his belongings.

That night she fell asleep on her apartment couch, on her side, her arms folded close, aching with emptiness collapsing like a glove dropped unawares, empty, into a blank and dreamless sleep.

"Can you tell me how to preserve the roses?" Julia asked the gardener. His name, she'd found out, was Palmer. She stood in the middle of the garden, surveying it, as if considering going to work herself.

"I don't know how really," he said and stopped his pruning for a moment. Palmer was such an odd man. He always seemed glad to be working, and equally glad to stop and speak with anyone, leaning, almost coyly, on the tip of his hoe. "But when I know I will be away from the roses, I collect the petals. Then I lay them on paper and turn them for a few days. Then I put them in a bowl. They keep that way for weeks."

"Do they have a musky smell?" Julia asked.

"No," he said. "No, it is a sweet fragrance. Their aroma is strong for quite a while."

"But you don't know about potpourri? Like an oil to add, to keep them longer?" she asked.

"I haven't really studied it," he said. "But I know with the perfume of the roses, the process is to preserve the alcohol and not the oil, if that helps," he said.

"Hmm . . ." Julia said. "So you just turn them, then?"

"Yes, on a piece of newspaper," he showed the sweeping motion of turning the petals with his hand and forearm. "Just keep turning them. Then put them in a bowl."

"Thank you," she said, gathered her coat around her and started home. Something was breaking in her when she thought of the gardener, like a glass globe inside. The edges took her by surprise.

The next day she hurried toward the rose garden, nervous and out of breath. What was it exactly? She didn't know. Somehow her peace was seeping out, but she didn't know from where. She didn't go directly inside the gate, but walked around until her breath calmed. She didn't like to enter hurriedly; it was not right to break the frail mood of the garden. She walked around the hedge. On her second turn, she saw the gardener sitting on a bench inside a domed alcove, eating an apple. First, he took a bite and spat it onto the ground. Then he ate the rest, biting and chewing, then biting again. His eyes narrowed each time he bit into the fruit. He threw the core onto the ground and wiped his mouth with his sleeve.

Julia stood in her mother's mohair coat. "Sea-foam green," her mother had called it. She was perfectly still, watching him. Waiting. Her enormous light eyes fixed on him in a way she would have never normally, eyes too large, unnaturally convex. Her chin drew to a point, her tiny mouth like a cat's, but slightly open. She walked away without entering the garden. He was the one.

She waited for Palmer outside the garden, then she asked him. And when he followed her home, where she had done nothing, made no special preparation and when he was with her, she was not thinking of him, although she was aware of his body's smoothness and weight; she was thinking of Jonathan's funeral. She had allowed no black and no flowers, asking instead for balloons and toys, and that they be sent to the children of those who came. She wore a lavender dress, and received everyone from the satin brocade armchair. She had worn a veil, a gift from Clare, so she could keep from her vision all who did not love him. She was smiling.

During this time she was more beautiful than she had ever been; she even let them say so. But if anyone wore black, she sent them away. Only pinks, reds, oranges, pale purples, the colors he loved, were permitted. And, of course, no tears.

Another time in the garden at night, when she refused Palmer's jacket, preferring the sensations of dew on her body, which she regarded as a kind of nectar they both understood and which made her feel less thievish, she was thinking that the roses that evening were very fine. It was all right. It was exactly right.

One morning, the neighbors woke her, arguing. "Get ready," a man's voice shouted. "'cause we're going to church!" She could tell the man was in the hall, banging on his apartment door. There was no answer but he kept hitting the door and screaming, "We're going to church. Better get ready."

As she lay there, she realized that she was going to have a child. She knew it. The doctors had been wrong when they said Jonathan could be the only one. She went into her bathroom carrying her secret and stared into nearly empty medicine cabinet, then closed it so that she could see the mirror. The man kept shouting and banging on the door, "We're going to church. Are you ready?" Her neighbor's anger, his noise, could not penetrate her calm. He could not touch her.

She wouldn't tell Palmer. He might be frightened, might think she wanted something. She believed he often went with women. There was no need for him to ever know. She had decided everything. She would stay here for a while. She would go back to work. She had a telephone installed, made inquiries, sent queries. Her resume had to be updated.

Palmer noticed a change in Julia. Her expression was less heavy, her face less drawn. The cynical laugh had disappeared. She began making lunch for him. She watched him eat while he rested on the stone bench. She liked watching him. Or he came to her apartment on days when the grounds were soggy.

One day she prepared hot tamales and corn bread in her apartment and brought them to him, explaining this had been her favorite childhood meal. She told him about stealing to-

matoes from the garden and seasoning them with coarse salt
from the cow shed. While they were drinking coffee, Palmer
told Julia that he thought she was lovely.

"Don't say that, ever." Her tone was deadly. She began
clearing the plates and carrying them into the kitchen.

After a pause, he followed her into the kitchen and sat on a tall
stool. He waited until the hissing of the water stopped. "We both
tend our gardens, don't we? Except yours is a private garden, only
for grieving, a locked garden." His manner was matter-of-fact.

She studied him, to be sure he was not angry, as if testing
that her own rancor found no counterpart in him. She had to
be sure. She strained to believe that he was not going to turn
on her, to do something unpredictable.

Julia dried her hands and walked into the living room. She
sat on the couch and patted a place beside her, although when
he joined her, she did not look at him. She spoke with effort,
as if she had no air. "I will never be pure enough." Her words
dragged.

"Your son," he said.

She seemed to be translating from another language in
which she would have known what to say into a language where
she had only a few words to tell him a very long story. She spoke,
distractedly, as though relating a dream she did not understand.

She told him about the woman speeding, talking to her
friend, paying no attention, not even braking until ... he'd
been run over on the road like a dog.

"He looked at me once, then closed his eyes. I stopped
cars in the road and said 'Breathe for him. Breathe. Breathe.' I
showed them how. And they did it. But it was no good."

She possessed every detail. The police. The doctors. The funeral. She hoarded the details. She had told no one. No one could discuss. No one could whisper. She made a language for what really happened. The others could not be permitted to see inside the coffin, though she kept having it opened, putting in stuffed animals, paper flowers, and finally, the cup from which he drank, a pottery cup that Jake had made. She allowed no one to see his body or describe his body. When she finished putting everything in, she signaled and they closed it, carried it, lowered it in the ground and she climbed down into the grave and lay on the coffin.

"We lay so close," Julia said, "so many nights."

As she spoke to Palmer, she remembered. And his bones, broken … his eyes, long surprised ovals which seemed to tilt forward, whose spirals showed every shade from green through blue, his eyes had opened and looked at her. He had tried to come to her but couldn't. This could not be. There was no one to breathe life into him. Though she remembered that he had pointed to the coral-colored flower, then to the same coral of the sky. She understood, but she could never forgive the woman in the speeding car. Therefore, she would never be pure enough.

"Blap," Julia said. "That's what'll happen if you go near the road. Blap. Blap." She smiled. "My husband said that to Jonathan once. He's got a funny word for everything. He doesn't talk about Jonathan."

Julia stayed inside now, ordering her groceries again, listening, being still. She was not pregnant. Palmer did not come by. One night she set her clock back an hour, slept an hour later, and rose into a day that would darken early. While separating her winter from her summer clothes, she began thinking about the garden. She imagined that it might be closing soon and she wanted to see it again. Julia put on her mohair coat, her gloves, and walked once more to the garden. It was crowded.

"This might be your last day," a visitor said to the gardener. There were two gardeners, then four, with newspapers and white foil, scampering around, decapitating the roses and inserting the stems into trays with water cups, passing them out to the visitors.

"Supposed to get down to twenty tonight," the visitor said to Palmer, who whistled.

Yes, Julia thought, and *Desconsuelo* will mourn alone all winter, steeped in the luxury of her stony moment. Today, she mourns the passing of the garden.

"Hello, Palmer," she said, and felt shy.

Palmer stopped his work and turned to her. She watched his handsome rodent's face. "How have you been?" he said.

"I'm all right," Julia said.

It had rained, so when Julia bent to smell a fully-bloomed white Pascali, a cold drop traced her lips which she parted and drank. But no one saw.

In her apartment, Vera was waiting to be fed, and after she had eaten, Julia called to her. "Vera! Kitty!" The fluffy white cat jumped onto the couch then stretched out on Julia's chest and stomach. She would go back to the farm. To Jake. Maybe. Or maybe not back to a man who could not speak his own child's name. Maybe not. Vera purred and Julia felt her lightness and heat, the vibration of her purring, as the cat lay there warm and soft and light, like a mink.

I Am Losing Everything

I LOST MY INHERITANCE in the streets of Somerville. I've invited another man into my house.

Rocks? he asks. *You don't have rocks?*

He drinks my bourbon, slow-melting amber, sipping honeys ripened especially for him. We are watching the Nixon/Kennedy debates from 1960. They are speaking in whole paragraphs, the King's English, instead of perserverating bumper-sticker bytes with puppet-like gestures intended to reach the American people. Who are these people, these American people?

He toasts the TV, says, *They had a lot of class back then.*

Now which class might that be? I say they have a lot of class *now*, a class so stratospherically high they can't see what's underfoot, the struggle and noise, the dirty and unkempt. Now *that's* class! I am losing everything.

I have lost my glasses, I unpack boxes and boxes, what to keep, what to throw away, slide book after book onto the shelves, the lifespan of silk worms, the atavistic fables, particle accelerators. Time snakes by me like fluid subway trains. Without my glasses, the world approaches and recedes, I can't think at all clearly, I'm rather un*focused,* a bit snowed under.

My teeth are falling out, my hands full of fillings, molars and rubber tubes, I return them to their sockets, everything feels so big in there, tongue like a fiber-optic camera, surveys the collapsed scaffolding. I have a craving for paint chips and bits of plastic; I am lacking something, some mineral.

I see people on a yacht with thick hair, Bermuda shorts, deck shoes. They're thinking about the way the sky meets the sea, how the blues vibrate together, their skin tanned and fragrant, pink nails with perfect half moons at the cuticle. Someone scrubs their sinks, broils their steaks, no clutter in their houses, no scribbled scraps of paper, no bits of blood-stained skin curled and blackened in the corners. It takes a dozen lives to live one of the lives on this yacht sailing straight for the horizon. You have to own a country for life to be this simple. You have to use up everything.

I find my glasses under the driver's seat, fish them out, hoping to free them without crushing them. Now it's all buried under overdue notices, phone bills with false charges I'll have to dispute, medical bills from laboratories I've never heard of, eyes of caged and starving tigers. Every day, a man in boots antagonizes the tiger, machines its spirit into ball bearings sliding out of control. With $25, they tell me, I can stop this man, the number is circled in red, but the phone rings, the word *unknown* appears on the receiver. I don't know her, but she seems to know me very well.

She tells me to reach inside my shoulder, the frail lining of cartilage that houses the head of the humerus, a delicate mouth holding the living egg, *You don't need that,* she whispers. And it's true, my life is full of things I'm not sure I need, tubes and needles drawing out marrow, nerves, oxygen.

I reach inside my shoulder and pull out the cartilage and take a bite. I have always loved cartilage and connective tissue. But now my arms will not have the most mobile joint in the body, winding up to throw a baseball or grenade, one hand scoops a lost baby, the other shoots its mother; oh, we don't leave behind our wounded. I am losing the structure.

Rocks? he says, the atoms of his touch heavy as plutonium, *Got any rocks? Yeah, they had class, a lot of class back then.*

My house is falling, parts of my body, time whooshes by like blue racer snakes, I've lost the people deepest in me that held up the columns, my twins, my merged identities. I lose scraps of paper, important numbers, but maybe it's all here, Byzantine links weaving back to the whole, shouts from the street, a shard of laughter, a girl buys me chocolate, wraps me in her jacket as we walk in the leaves like autumn at Ricky Nelson's house, and for a moment I'm okay; for a moment, I love everything.

I work a problem inside my head, how to forgive, how to forgive, I wake at four in the morning, shake my head, *No, no, no, you have to do better.* Are you my silenced sister, my lost twin brother, a broken tiger mother in a box marked *urgent?*

I turn myself inside out, empty into the world's edges, which cuts off bits and savors, melts and sucks till I am see-through thin, waiting for that last crackling occlusion, when I when I lose structure. For life to be this simple, to find anything, to love anyone, I've got to lose and lose and lose.

No Surprise

I KNEW IN WALES, in the stone cottage, on the moist July morning, when I touched one of my old friend Emma's confection-like breasts while she was sleeping, I knew how lonely I had become.

So it was no surprise in Amsterdam, in the light of the pink lamp, in the leather booth of the café I occupied every afternoon, attended by the same young waiter, no surprise when he asked me to a hotel. He suggested amiably, half-joking. His body immediate under the thin waiter's uniform. I thought about it, would have gone, had he not been so honest about having a wife. I thought of her in their tiny channel apartment, painted white and gray and Dutch blue. I imagined that she worked outside the city, commuting daily to one of the vast flower farms.

When the hotel keep, large-boned, particular, willing to spend long mornings talking in the small garden that let off the huge day room, the one with the most wood carvings, when he closed his hand over mine, it was no surprise that I could be convinced that life could be a simple, joyful, "Yes, Josef, of course."

And because I was so hungry, I did go to his bed where I sighed and ate toast and peaches from around the corner. It was the season and we always chose the best ones, fat with ripe sugar.

From his bed I could count eight faces, carved from the same wood as the dark molding. Human faces repeated around the room in a variety of expressions, like characters in a medieval play, each about the size of a man's hand. A Jewish family had built the house, he said. The sculpted wooden faces, traditional Jewish bourgeoisie decoration of the period, and so it was no surprise that the original deeds had disappeared.

"A guest once ran into the street crying, when she saw them." Josef said. "She'd known without a doubt. Recognized the style of the carving."

"That's true, isn't it?" I said. "So many things are apparent once you know what to look for."

I had been so famished and so it was no surprise, as I wandered the cobbled streets, that I began to believe I could dwell finally on the inside, where the lamps shone in the handsome parlors, and no longer be always the stranger.

To believe that he'd meant, when he whispered beneath the quilts patch-worked from velvet dresses and woolen trousers, "I would go anywhere in the world to be with you."

I watched as he peeled and seeded cucumbers, carved the dense bread into gaunt slices. He tended the knives, his right hand applying the blade, the left steadying the steel.

I noticed the skill and tenderness of his left hand, how the right hand insisted and mauled until one night I slapped him when he wouldn't stop when I'd said stop. Then I could see on his face the other times he'd been slapped, times when he could not simply leave the way I did then, my morning walks extending late into afternoon.

The ether between us began to shift and we couldn't prevent it, although we tried but could not. I tried harder because my heart was perhaps not so divided, not so in need of clear distinctions—right and wrong, passion or aversion, and because I was more disappointed, having not quite seen it coming.

By then he'd become critical. I'd placed the chairs improperly, I'd not understood when he'd called to tell me, "Stay out of my room," and I thought he'd meant come in. It was as though he had been calling and calling and couldn't bear having been answered.

By then, we weren't sleeping. I went back to the room where I'd first stayed as a guest, though twice more we spent afternoons—with peaches and cognac—after I'd come back from the lamp-lit café attended by the solicitous young waiter in the thin uniform. In the single room, I realized I wanted to bathe, that I no longer wanted Josef's residue on my skin.

I left the room immaculate, so that even he could not complain, as though I had never been there, except for a coaster, advertising a local beer, the top one from a stack of four.

I don't call it a mistake, don't say this was the wrong thing, don't regret that there is no picture of him, with his gray-blond curls and his broad provincial face, because I remember everything I need to remember about Josef. I regret not knowing all the carved faces.

I've heard that sometimes porous surfaces, such as cloth or wood, absorb events and sound waves over time. I want to know what those wooden eyes may have shown me, about what those wooden lips may have spoken, about the solitary hotel keep who houses the spirits of wanderers, about the family that disappeared. Had they joined hands around the lamp-lit table, the family that disappeared as though never there?

I want to read the carved faces with my fingertips the way Josef did as he polished them, touching their expressions of sadness and of ire. Had they known what to look for? Had they been surprised?

Jesus and the Sineaters

MY MOTHER SAID I reminded her of my cat, Arcadio: lost and blind. After the explosion, I found him by the road. His jaw hung down, drooling blood in the weeds. His eyes wide and blind, cars roaring past him, inches from his face. Gradually, his forepaw drew inward, curling to his chest; his head nodded and nodded, *yes, yes.* Lost and blind, she said. For God's sake, put him to sleep. Everyone agreed. I know their reasons are the same as those who wish I would wear pants to cover my scars. Such things should not be intruded upon the eye. But he wanted to live. I knew. I let him live. I wear my cotton shorts in this endless summer. Children stare. Stroke me, wanting to know if the wounds still hurt. Their mothers tell them not to be rude, not to look. Their fathers step forward bearing their anger like a dark flower.

Arcadio roars. He hammers at the door with his good paw. At last he learns to open it. He slings himself onto the platform I built for him by the window to catch the morning sun.

He is an old man, punishing his body for having betrayed him. He bangs it around, giving the impression that he is insensible to pain. Motion is a skewed maneuver for Arcadio. He moves by spinning slowly in circles. If he wants to die, he will stop eating. Wanting, not wanting to die.

We lived along the strip of road two miles from the sea. My brother and his wife, Pinky, making cabinets, my parents in their bungalow and myself in the house with the orchards. After the firestorm, our skin melted off like shredding silk. We wandered away from each other, hands stretched in front of us, sleepwalkers, stunned and wordless. We trembled like compass needles, dazed, but on course—East North South West, Brother Mother Sister Father, away from the imploding magnetic center. It has been nine months since we buried Pinky in the town cemetery. Six months since my brother joined the carnival at Clover Point. Four months since my father began his wandering.

Now I drink only orange juice and salt. Equal parts, mixed in a glass. The day nurse said that was the only thing to save me. On Thursdays, I make the slow journey down the charred road to the store at the end of the road. Twelve blood oranges. Iodized salt. Iodine is good for light-skinned people who have moved inland. Half orange juice, half salt and nothing else. I buy no other food in case it is contaminated or drugged. I can't allow anything to alter my tenuous grip. The man at the register folds his arms. One day he will make small talk. Will smile at me.

Outside the store, the men smoke on the long benches and shake their heads. Mr. Tarkington nods as I walk by. His smile is a wince. He says it was like a spontaneous combustion. The others say it looked like an A-bomb, the way the wall of fire climbed up and flared out and left a crater big as a canyon, the sound quaking down in the core of their bodies, though it was happening miles off.

I remember the detonation. The flash, then the laughter which landed later, everyone's relief, daggers pocking my yard. For weeks, the newspaper wrote of scales and numbers, if there had been ten thousand or only twenty five. What number could be justified? What number of us could be traded for numbers of them. But how can something of infinite value be added or multiplied?

I consider this on the way back from the store, past the leaning houses. From the rise of the third hill, I can see my house curled in among the sassafras and cypress. It is still proud, whole. It does not betray me. When the wind from the firestorm entered our houses, it left the pattern of its path on our bodies. My legs and arms, my mother's arms and hands, my brother's slender back, and my father's face. My father, who'd been wrapped in his hammock for a nap. We kept the charred places clean and red until they turned into flat scabs of leather. Now they crack with every move; the blood trickles and dries on our good skin. Or heal, sticking with the tight glue of scars, arms welding to torsos, joints stiffening.

After the firestorm, and the hospital, I wanted to stay indoors. I faded down to two green eyes housed in bone, dipped in pale shadow. Women envied me or knew I was dying. Some prepared feasts, spoke in hushed tones. But I couldn't speak or eat. Nothing could go in or out. One hundred ten, one hundred, ninety-five, eighty-five … I couldn't think. I would balloon into the middle of the ocean, a spider on her silk, draped in scarves and heavy boots. No one would see me. I would bow my back and recede through time. Last month, Arcadio disappeared for three days. I found him in the orchard, spinning, nodding, *yes, yes.*

Later, he disappeared completely and for the first time I was afraid. Without his anger and heat, I was hollowed. I lay beneath the trees, listening for his rustle and howl as the bruises deepened on the sun-colored apples. I breathed in their fragrance, a force growing more solid, seeking my attention.

My house was empty. I could not fill it by myself. Night filtered through rooms I could not defend. My father brought his friends in, setting up shop one day while I walked for blood oranges. They swung open the heavy doors so that alarmed cattle trampled through, butting into shelves, licking the walls with their sticky tongues. The men shot through the limbs of the sassafras to scatter the starlings.

"Ooooooweee!" They shouted, gripping the gun stocks with their cold hands. Almost instantly, the starlings crowded the limbs again, calling to one another in their strange razzmatazz tongue like spinning noisemaker toys.

Later, my mother came for my father, shooing the men away. "Trash," she said. I remind her of my cat, she repeated. "We are a family," she said. Her elbows are webbed to her side, circumscribing her gestures. "If we weaken, we are defeated." Her voice pinched higher and tighter in her throat. "Your life is wrong," she said. "You drop into madness like a bird drops into flight. You are denying reality."

"Your reality."

"No. I understand the laws of nature."

Spare me the details.

"Here are a few of my laws."

A six means death. Thirteen, once a strong, dry, yellow number, now means danger, unexpected tragedy. If I leave my shallow breathing in the house while I take up watch in the orchard, disaster may be averted. A full moon means a night full of children's voices, a cradle of moon means bodies housed in skin in a world more dense than they. Don't worry, Mother, I no longer require that you understand. These are injected meanings, my scant order.

When my brother is not working at Clover Point, he is a mystic in town. Angels fly into the sickrooms where he ministers. They loom above him, seven feet tall. Gold bands flow to a point on their foreheads. Jesus smiles at him over the dying. He and Jesus do not speak. It is their secret.

Jesus was a sineater. However, I know many. We congregate in astral bodies. We lose everything and more. Each time we lose, we must pour back love. "Do you want to be healed?" we say. "Of course," they answer. Yes, they nod. Yes. Yes. All day we listen. Sineaters, embracing sorrow. We conduct it down, the silver current of death, down the lightning rod, harmless into the ground. "Easy," we say. "It's all right." We open the blood. We let the poison.

Their coming is unpredictable—people from town. Some I recognize, others have traveled a long distance and must stay the night. When the priest comes, he explains his disadvantage: what of the man who confesses that he wants to kill his wife, that to kill her would give him pleasure? "I've taken the oath of secrecy," he says. How can he protect her body? How can he protect either soul? He wipes his forehead with a white cloth and sleeps in the front room with the alder tree at the window.

There is a couple who arrive separately, explaining how they must leave each other, but each time one tries, the other follows, pleading. Each time they must do something worse to prove they mean it. She claws him, tears his clothes, he throws her rings into the sea. One day he follows her down the narrow path at dusk; the next, she follows him. "We can think of nothing else," she says. In the moonlight, her hair rises around her head, a wreath of electricity. There are those who come to gather sacred apples from the orchard.

Sometimes at night they rush the land, thieves on every hand. I am spun in the gears of their dreams or pinned while they rummage through brother's sacred hearts, looking for a cigarette. I absorb, gluttonous, all the gorgeous confession. I am brim with unchosen sorrow.

The fire eater has a trick. He draws kerosene from the torch so the fire consumes the fuel on his hand or tongue. Before his flesh becomes fuel, he dips his unscathed hand in water. Can sineaters learn tricks or do they swallow the flames and later break out in scars?

I'm not Jesus, but I get the picture. First despair, then tunnels of light. That's the algebra of it. But I never wanted it. Maybe this is the path to wisdom, vision. But it's not what I had in mind.

Brother charted my father's wanderings and found an ellipse. He unfurled the scroll with charts and diagrams. "His path," he said, "resembles that of the moon around the earth, the earth around the sun." With his thin rod of polished wood, he pointed, explaining why we see the moon in its phases. "It's not the shadow of the earth," he said, "But the angle of light." His eyes are so bright, it hurts to meet them. Under his cape of stars, he hides his corrugated back.

Brother sips another dram. He milks a torch, then touches his lips and spits a flame. Again, a blue flame floats from his palms. He dips his hand and waters his garden of distractions. Jesus works for him.

Tonight the orchard is silent; the house, empty but for a thin inhaling. Together we hold our breath, hold in the heavy scent of the apples. Walking, I see a swirling in the leaves, then Arcadio making turns, slow circles. His fur is dry and thin, his skin hangs loose on his bones. When I take him in the darkened house, he eats and sleeps until he is able to rage again. For this time, we are safe, to live on our thoughts, on oranges and salt, and one day soon, the dark fruits of the orchard— among the trees where days do not move forward, but dissolve. We will breathe and sift relief from the famished air.

Instructions From Men

MARION SQUINTED through the screened-in porch of her Uncle Tudor's house at the men playing horseshoes. When they finished, they were supposed to set up for the Easter egg hunt. Although Marion had read about Easter egg hunts in her *What Next?* fifth-grade reading book, she'd never actually been on one. She'd made colored eggs out of construction paper for the bulletin board and imagined herself chasing around the yard with other children collecting decorated eggs in a straw basket with friends who rolled in the long grass and traded their prizes. There were no thistles to step on like there were in Uncle Tudor's yard and no bratty cousins. This afternoon, she'd seen Grandma Slade fussing through the house carrying bags of secrets and she had to admit she was excited.

"Close!" Uncle Jessie shouted. His horseshoe dropped heavily in front of the stake and scattered up a tiny dust cloud.

"Well, close counts in horseshoes and atom bombs, now don't it?" Uncle Tudor said.

"Tudor, you're a card," Uncle Jessie said and clapped the dust from his hands.

"I wish Bill could be here with us today," Uncle Skeeter said and bowed his head. Marion's father, Bill Slade, was off in the Korean War. Last week she'd gotten a package in the mail from Korea with little boxes of soft candy and toys made with painted straw. It surprised Marion that her father had thought of her.

The April sun reflected from the men's white shirts and illuminated the tufts of new grass, thick with dandelions and violets. Inside, her mother and aunts were cooking Easter dinner. Marion's mother and Aunt Pi both smoked Lucky Strikes inside the kitchen, so Aunt Doris kept fanning the back door and hollering "Shoooee!" Marion's mom liked to say how Doris and Skeeter were kept extra busy showing everybody right from wrong. When Aunt Doris fanned the door, the sweet smells of baking and cigarette smoke wafted outside.

Cigarette smoke made Marion happy. It meant zipping around the county in the car with her mother. They raced down the winding roads listening to the Top Twenty and singing as loud as they could. Marion thought she had a terrible voice, but her mother said singing cleansed the soul. Marion knew about the importance of a cleansed soul from church, so she sang along with her mother. *Just me and her, yeah, we gotta get back to that Sugar Shack, oh honey . . .*

They whipped in and out of side roads and blind turns while her mother laughed then cried. Marion knew the crying had something to do with her father. Marion could see her parents were a handsome couple—her mother's dresses rustling around her slender calves, her father's rayon shirts open at the throat, walking arm-in-arm at parties. It seemed to Marion that they wanted to go forward with some extraordinary plan but weren't sure how to go about it. She didn't understand why she and her mother had to wait outside the Half Moon Lounge for her father to come out if all her mother wanted to do was fight with him. Twice, she and her mother had sped off together in the car only to come back after midnight and bang on the door to be let in. She understood that it was necessary for her mother to be with her father, no matter how it was.

"You're winning, Jess." Tudor marked the horseshoe score on the concrete cistern lid with blue carpenter's chalk.

Marion liked Uncle Tudor's red-and-white checked shirt, his creased jeans and elaborate cowboy boots. Tudor had surprised everyone after his wife left him, by fixing up the farm and starting a real estate business in town.

"Looks like you were just hiding your light under a barrel," Marion overheard Uncle Skeeter say. If Marion was going to buy a house, Tudor would be who she'd pick to sell it to her.

Just then, Jessie's daughter Candace prissed up and asked Tudor to fix her sash. When Tudor cocked his head, the sun flashed in his sleek, dark hair. Marion bolted through the door and raced past her cousins. "Last one to the barn is a punk," she called and they all chased after her.

Uncle Jessie's four wore blue-and-white: seersucker suits for the boys, circle skirts for Candace and baby Shannon. The boys each held one of Shannon's hands and pulled her up so high she barely touched the ground. Candace skipped. Skeeter's son, Seth, dragged along pale and sulky like he wanted pity for acting half dead.

Marion touched the splintery barn door then turned and stood with her arms outstretched to represent the finish line. Each one tagged her then crashed against the barn. They'd been to church, so the boys' hair was slicked to the side with Lilac Vegetal. Marion was glad she'd been spared the rick-rack and stand-out slips like Candace and Shannon had to wear, but she wished she could have changed into corduroy pants before they'd driven all the way out Wade's Mill Road.

"Seth's a rotten egg!" Candace shrieked as she broke through the imaginary finish line.

"Am not," Seth said. He kicked at a dried-up cow pie and chewed idly at his fingernails. Seth was so spoiled by Uncle Skeeter and Aunt Doris that he could barely tie his own shoes.

"First one back sees Peter Rabbit," Marion called and raced toward the house. The cousins ran halfway, then stopped to play with the model cars and toys they'd left upended in the grass. Candace waved her hand in front of her face as though she were about to faint. "Come here, Shannon," she said, picking up her pink hula hoop. "Count how many times I make it go around without falling." Marion sat on the bottom step with her chin in her hands.

The uncles were up on the porch, leaning back against the house in cane-bottomed chairs with their legs spread. Tudor and Uncle Jessie were rolling cigarettes and drinking Schlitz beer from bottles while Skeeter pretended not to notice. Uncle Skeeter was a preacher for the Church of Christ downtown, where Marion and her mother sometimes went.

They had to be silent except for when they sang, because the Bible said women were not allowed to speak in church, even in Sunday school class. When Uncle Skeeter preached, he seemed to go into a trance. He paced and implored the Holy Spirit to come into the building. His giant lustrous wave of hair heaved back and forth. "I entreat you. I admonish you," he'd chant. "Have pity on these poor sinners."

Marion liked the songs they sang at Skeeter's church, the low steady voices of the men and the high quaking women's voices, her mother's voice singing harmony somewhere in the middle. The congregation sang without a piano because of something else it said in the Bible about not playing musical instruments in church. This worried Marion because her favorite daydream was of living alone in a tree house and being a guitar player who wore blue jeans and cowboy boots like her Uncle Tudor's. People gathered to listen while she played and sang with a voice like Phil Everly. Now Marion wondered if those thoughts meant she was a lost sheep.

On the porch, Uncle Tudor was telling stories about one of his real estate clients who ordered gold bathroom fixtures. "Fourteen K, swear to God." Tudor pressed a palm over his heart and Uncle Jessie laughed so hard he had to hold his big stomach to keep from hurting himself. Uncle Jessie was so fat, bib overalls was the only thing that fit him anymore.

Marion's mother said that it was scary how much the Slade side of the family seemed to have so many dominant genes. Marion knew about genes from school, so she felt she understood some mystery when they were all together with their eerie gray eyes, high foreheads and overlong, loose-jointed limbs.

All of Grandma Slade's sons had joined the service, except for Skeeter, who had a skin disorder. At six foot five, her father was the tallest enlisted man ever to come out of Wyandot County. She liked it that now all they had of him were thin, striped envelopes in the mail.

Marion passed shyly in front of the men, headed for the kitchen to help her mother.

"Hey, Mary," Uncle Tudor said. He always shortened women's names—he'd called his own wife Mary, too, instead of Marie, even though it made her mad.

Tudor patted his knee and Marion eased herself onto his lap. She was wearing the same dress she'd worn last Easter, lavender with tulips appliquéed around the skirt. She'd modeled it for her father last year as he'd surveyed her from the couch. "Make sure you sit like a lady today," he'd said. He was wearing a satin robe and eating orange sections. "How come you're not going to church?" Marion wanted to know. "Because I've got to stay here and wait for Peter Rabbit."

He'd reached over to pinch her knee, but she'd jerked it away just in time. She knew this meant there would be an Easter basket with purple foil and cellophane grass when she got home, but it also probably meant a long afternoon riding her bike up and down the road while her parents argued. She'd walked away from her father, her shoes clacking on the hardwood floors. "I don't believe in Peter Rabbit," she said and when she was out of earshot whispered, "And I don't believe in God." This year her dress was too tight and this morning she had to hold her breath to get it buttoned. She wore a sweater to hide the soft mounds of her breasts.

"I heard your mama say you made the super honor roll," Tudor said. "Now what in the world is that?"

"All A's," Marion answered. She adjusted her skirt and stared at her patent-leather shoes. It was hard for her to meet Tudor's gaze, even though they had the same clear gray eyes with little flares of violet.

"And what about a boyfriend?" Uncle Jessie leaned toward her, wiggling his wiry eyebrows.

Marion shook her head no. There was one boy she liked, Phillip Peyton, a seventh grader with curly hair who played on the baseball team. No one knew though.

Grandma Slade pushed through the back door and let it slam. She smoothed wisps of her hair toward the bun at the nape of her neck. "Come on," she said. "I think I hear Peter Rabbit coming." She marched across the yard to ring the dinner bell. Grandpa Slade had died two years ago, but Uncle Jessie said that hadn't weakened his mama. She could still pound the dinner bell loud enough to call home the prophets. "Round up these children, Tudor," she said. She wiped flour from her hands onto her apron. "This shindig was your idea."

Uncle Tudor led Marion and her cousins down the porch stairs and across the backyard. Inside the barn, light fell through the slots between the planks and onto the dirt floor. The coolness and the quiet of the barn hushed the other children. Along one wall stood a wooden loading wagon, flanked by a tobacco setter with rusting twin seats and a V of long rails stacked with hickory tobacco sticks. It made Marion dizzy to look up and think of men crawling around those rails hanging tobacco up to cure.

Every year there was a story of someone falling and breaking an arm or leg. Last year a boy from the high school had fallen from the top bent and ended up in a wheelchair. It made Marion extra careful, thinking how one moment could change your whole life.

This time of year there was no tobacco in the barn, but a sweet wild scent still made the air heavy, especially in the stripping room where Uncle Tudor lined them up against the wall. The rest of the barn had spaces so air could circulate around the tobacco, but Uncle Tudor had nailed up sheets of plywood in this room. That way, the potbellied stove could keep them warm while they stripped tobacco into grades for the January market.

"Pretty dress," Uncle Tudor said to Marion in a voice that made her think of chocolate. She knew he was standing close enough so that if either of them moved, they'd be touching. "Now you all stay in here and don't peek," he said. "If you do, I'll tan all your hides."

When Uncle Tudor left the barn, he propped a hickory stick against the door from the outside. The boys picked on Candace, telling her the bogeyman was coming after her. Shannon asked too many questions: Would they be candy eggs or real ones? If they were real, was she supposed to eat them like candy? Real eggs? Was it just the shells with all the insides sucked out like when the weasels sneaked in Grandma Slade's hen house? Seth complained that he didn't like hiding in some old dirty barn waiting on candy. He got all the candy he wanted at home. One of Jessie's boys reckoned that's why Seth's teeth rotted out of his head. "All of you, hush,"

Marion said. She squeezed Shannon's hand so hard she started to whimper. "Oh, I'm sorry, honey." Marion kissed the top of Shannon's head. They listened to the whispering outside the barn and rustling in the grass.

Marion sighed and adjusted the waistband of her dress. She didn't know if she was chubby or plain old fat; her mother said she just had a little baby fat, and that it would fall off by the time she finished junior high. Marion doubted that because she was always hungry. She couldn't keep away from the sugared spice drop candy her mother kept in the satin glass dish. On every trip through the house, Marion lifted the lid with her breath held and took one to dissolve in her mouth. Then there would be just a heap of sugar dust at the bottom of the dish and she'd have to wait a whole week for more. She decided that the shelves in her tree house would hold an endless supply of everything she wanted to eat.

"Look who's come!" Grandma Slade shouted and swung open the barn doors. She handed out paper bags to the cheering cousins. The sunlight made Marion's eyes ache and when she dashed into the yard, she tripped on a root and almost fell. Rolls of pastel crepe paper outlined the area of the hunt. As her eyes adjusted, she could see colored bits tucked into the green tufts of grass and propped up foil-wrapped bunnies. The cousins all hollered, bolting in every direction, but Marion moved carefully, full of intent. She found a blue egg with a gold star painted on it and a nest of malted milk balls. She found Hershey's kisses, jelly beans and yellow marshmallow chicks. Best were finding the eggs, whole and solid and painted with zigzags, crescent moons or little faces. She couldn't imagine who in her family would have taken the time to do such a thing. She found one egg with a purple kitten painted on the side and realized with a start that it had been painted by the only person in her family who knew how to draw—her mother. She placed her treasures gently in the bottom of her bag. She imagined Peter Rabbit disappearing over the hill to the next farm with his wagonload of surprises.

When Marion wandered close to the house, she could smell corn bread and boiled cabbage with something sweet and rich mingled in. She heard Uncle Jessie's raised voice, something about the war and President Eisenhower. Marion knew by the voice that he would be calling into the kitchen for another beer and that Aunt Peggy would bring it out on a little tray with a glass and napkin. Her mother brought her father beer too—but when he asked, she'd stride across the porch, slap the bottle in his hand and ask him if his leg was broken.

Most of the cousins were scrambling to the far corner of the yard where balloons trailed down from the walnut tree. Marion was about to follow when she heard someone whisper, "Mary." When she looked up, she saw Uncle Tudor's face peer around the door to the stripping room. "Mary," he repeated, "Come here."

Marion clutched her bag and approached with a cautious smile. She was suddenly ashamed to have been seen romping in the yard. Maybe twelve was too old to be collecting eggs in the grass with a bunch of little kids. It occurred to her that maybe he'd saved back the best Easter surprise for her. She'd been told that getting older meant certain privileges, but so far it had only meant giving things up to the younger ones. Or maybe she and Uncle Tudor were going to play a prank on the others.

It was hard for her to see inside the dim barn, but she felt herself being lifted onto the low table where they laid out tobacco stalks to strip off their leaves. A sour beer smell pushed into her face. Uncle Tudor didn't say anything, but gently took the bag from her hand and set it beside her. He ducked his head outside the door for a moment, then closed it.

His voice was low, like a wood rasp. "Hug my neck," he said. When she did, he reached under her and removed her panties. Now she could see his eyes, narrowed and shining. He parted her knees with his hands and after a moment rubbed something heavy and stiff between her legs. Marion felt her face go red in the heavy dark of the barn, but she continued to hold her arms delicately around his neck and hoped this would be over soon. Above her uncle's low moan, Marion heard her cousins yelping in the yard and the murmur of adults in the background. She worried that one of the children might wander in here, thinking there were more treasures.

Something was forcing her to widen and when she flinched Uncle Tudor withdrew. He put his hand behind her head and pushed it gently toward him. "Open your mouth, Mary. That's right." He cupped her head in his hands to steady it while he moved. "All right." Then it seemed the man she knew as Uncle Tudor was no longer there, and she was afraid of suffocating, of dying in this barn inhaling the musk of tobacco and the foreign scent of her uncle up so close doing this secret thing. She imagined her mother flinging open the barn door and pouring in light and fury at her, demanding to know why her new underwear was on the floor. But her mother didn't come, there was only this clutching and hard motion until finally it was over and Uncle Tudor did something, peed maybe, on the dirt floor littered with last season's dry leaves.

Marion was embarrassed for him. When she heard Grandma Slade bang the dinner bell, she jumped off the table and searched unseeing along the dusty table for her underwear, grabbed them and felt for the tag to know front from back. She lost her balance and she pulled them over her shoes. Uncle Tudor fumbled for something, then handed her the bag. "If you tell," he said, in a still voice, "They'll send me far away." He reached in his pocket, then pressed something heavy and cool into her hand. Once in the light, she could see he had given her a silver dollar. It was more money than she'd ever owned all at once.

The crepe paper borders had blown out of shape and were tumbling in the yard. The cousins were playing chase around the house. Marion put the coin in her sock and broke across the lawn, joining them at a dead run. They all raced, yelling that they were Little Black Sambo's tiger, chasing its tail. They would run until they dissolved into butter for Sambo's hot cakes. "Into butter! Into butter!" They all shouted, with Marion shouting loudest till the dinner bell clanged the second time meaning come to the table now, then they'd collapsed, gasping in the yard.

All of Marion's favorite foods were arranged on a long table in the yard. There was potato salad, sliced tomatoes, briny cucumbers, corn pudding and cream pies. Two enormous platters heaped with some kind of fowl weighted the tablecloth at either end. The white cloth bucked with the breeze, and for a moment, Marion was afraid all the food would be thrown into the grass, but then they all gathered around the table stilling the breeze, bowing their heads while Uncle Skeeter asked the blessing. He thanked the Lord for the food and remembered Marion's father, hoping that he be protected until he was returned to his family. Marion rubbed the fabric of her dress between her fingers. Maybe awful things happened to you when you said you didn't believe in God. As they filled their plates, Uncle Jessie said he missed listening to his brother play the French harp. He said he could be playing it in Korea right now for all they knew.

The women gathered on a quilt under the oak tree and talked about what a good cook Aunt Doris was, that she always made the best fruitcake and Christmas pudding. Marion's mother and Aunt Pi always made fun of Aunt Doris behind her back. Marion guessed that being the good cook was a kind of consolation for not being one of them.

The cousins had a little table set up in the spotted shade of the walnut tree, but Marion sat on a low stump with her plate in her lap. Uncle Tudor sat with the men on the steps of the porch balancing plates piled with layers of food. Marion sliced into dark meat. This had been the sweet, rich aroma floating in the yard earlier, but she couldn't quite identify it. She glanced at her mother, who was dressed all in red linen with red fingernails and matching pumps looking for all the world like a movie star. When she asked her what kind of meat this was, her mother didn't answer. She was busy whispering something and giggling in Aunt Pi's ear.

"Mary, could you get me a beer?" Tudor asked from the porch step.

"I'll get it, Uncle Tudor," Candace said, jumping up.

"You can get me the next one, Candy," Tudor said.

When Marion handed Tudor the beer, he thanked her but his eyes held a look she couldn't place right then. His body seemed coiled in a way that made her want to get away, but which pulled at her at the same time. She thought of the repelling and attracting magnets experiments from school. At the small table, one of Jessie's boys was crying and the cloth was soaked with red Kool-Aid. And Shannon had what looked like the insides of a marshmallow bunny all matted in her hair. She wondered if what she'd done with Uncle Tudor meant she would have a baby. She hoped not. She wondered if this meant he loved her. She would keep the money in her hidden drawer with her Indian dolls and her Bible and her Valentine from Jimmy Peyton. She would keep it while it increased in value because it was much better to have a silver dollar than a dollar's worth of anything you could spend it on.

Later, Marion looked back on that day knowing three things that she didn't know then: one, that the look in Tudor's eyes was not love but an alloy of greed and fear—fear that she would tell, which she never did, no matter how many silver dollars he forced into her palm, how impossible it was for her either to refuse or spend them, how much he threatened or insisted or begged her forgiveness afterward, zipping his pants without looking at her. This greed abided steadfastly beneath a thick coat of charm, a combination which made him the most successful Realtor in the county.

Secondly, that she would not get the outfit her mother promised her on the drive back to town that day, because her father, home from Korea and spending evenings lounging at the Half Moon, said string ties and cowboy hats were not right for girls. After his return, she and her mother drove even faster down the country roads shouting out the Top Twenty—*I held her tight; I kissed her our last kiss*—till one afternoon the car slid into a ditch and Uncle Jessie had to tow them out with his wrecker. He shook his big shaggy head and remarked that they were both lucky to be alive. Marion's mother said that she didn't know about that.

One Sunday in the fall, Uncle Skeeter spoke of the beauty of silence in women and how they were supposed to take counsel and receive instructions from men. He paced the floor, slamming his fist on the podium, shaking his forefinger toward the congregation, raking his fingers through his dollop of hair. All of a sudden he stopped, his eyes lifted heavenward, his hands outstretched with autumn sun melting through them and onto his wooden platform and proclaimed, "I suffer not a woman to teach nor to usurp authority over the man, but to be in silence."

"Does Uncle Skeeter remind you of Elvis?" Marion asked her mom after they'd climbed into the car.

Her mother smiled and lit a cigarette. "Spitting image," she said, flooring the accelerator and kicking up gravel getting out of the lot.

They pulled into Jerry's and ordered chipped ham sandwiches and French fries, Marion's favorite. Marion was quiet, hoping her mother would talk. If she talked, maybe somehow Marion could figure things out in her own mind, but her mother seemed far away. Marion wanted to ask her questions, but she didn't know the right ones to ask. Instead, she watched the girls in uniforms and caps rush back and forth from the restaurant to the cars, balancing trays of food, change-makers strapped around their waists. She'd told her mom about liking Jimmy Peyton at school, and her mother looked at her all deadly and told her to be careful about the men. Marion thought maybe men were like spice drops and once you started with them, you couldn't stop no matter how sick it made you afterward.

The third thing, she found out from Grandma Slade. Since Marion was coming to Wade's Mill once a week to help Tudor with the books for his real estate business, her grandmother kept her up on family news. Candace and Shannon were taking ballet *which was a good thing because Candace was getting round as a barrel.* Seth had a little *snot-nosed girlfriend who whined as bad as he did.* Jessie's boys were in the hospital for some kind of special operation just for boys. "With Thanksgiving coming on, I got to laughing about something that happened last Easter." Grandmother Slade leaned close to Marion, as though imparting the most intimate of family secrets. "We had a little accident that day," she said. "Not ten minutes before dinner was ready, Aunt Pi had been flailing a kitchen match in one hand and holding her Lucky Strike in the other. Anyway, she'd backed into one of the platters of meat and knocked it plum into the dishwater. Don't you know Doris fished out ever last piece and rinsed the suds off. We dabbed them with towels, mixed them in with the rest and hoped no one would notice. We were so quiet that the men got restless and called after their dinner." Grandma Slade laughed and swatted a fly with a newspaper.

"Well, I didn't notice." Marion smiled as she gathered her school books from the kitchen counter, leaving half the slice of mince pie her grandmother had served her. "If there'd been a real problem, I'm sure Seth would have vomited up suds to get sympathy."

Her mother had been right, the baby fat was gone, she'd narrowed around her waist and filled out other places. Thirteen was being a teenager; it felt much older than being twelve. She was first in her class and the only one to have the nerve to say what atheists and agnostics were. Marion closed the back door and took a path through the snow toward Tudor's office. She knew Tudor would be waiting for her with a fire built and maybe a little present.

The reason she was so good with his books was the way she could arrange figures on paper. It was something she'd learned to do in her own mind. If you walked around something, you could get a new angle on it. If you put the facts together in a certain order, you could usually get them to be what you wanted, or at least something you could live with. After she finished the book, Tudor would draw the shade and offer her a Lucky Strike. When he reached forward to light it, she'd match his gray gaze with her own. It would be his hand that trembled.

Marion kicked the snow off her loafers outside the office. She remembered then that there had been something odd about the meat last Easter. She'd asked her mother twice if it were chicken or turkey. Or maybe quail.

When no one answered, Uncle Tudor had said, finally, "Well, Mary. What do you want it to be?" She'd considered a minute, thinking of her father hunting, bringing home a clutch of small birds, the tender, wild-tasting flesh. "Quail." Tudor winked. His glossy hair snared little rainbows in the sun. "Well, then, that's what it is."

Polyvinyl Chloride

I WEAR MY MOTHER'S SWEATER, her foundation makeup a beigey crud along the neckline. I smell *L'air du Temps* and the sensuality of her anger. I savor her traces, the dropped safety pins, the envelope corners with uncanceled postage stamps she intends to use, scattered on the Italian marble table. The marble holds a pattern like soft clay stirred through with blood and gold. She bought it at auction, its price one of her intimate secrets.

My mother owns a tattered collection of ceramic dolls, which she hung from the Christmas tree one year. It appeared as though an evil gang had ripped clothing from the doll children, forced poison down their exquisite porcelain throats. Some arms had slipped off, revealing loops of wire. Such is my mother's tree.

At some point, there is too much of my mother. The way she pulls me to her, squeezes till I say "Love you." The way her car seats are rimed with cigarette ashes and dog hair. I tug off her sweater. Though she is far more stylish, the soles of her high heels are made of leather too thin, their pitch too steep, the shoe backs only a strap.

I shift the hangers along the closet rail, searching for my father's white shirts, his khaki pants. Maybe there's one of those Johnny Carson suits, well-tailored gabardine with a gold-and-red tie, striped on the diagonal, full of happy potential, like a holiday.

"There we are," I whisper, squaring up the tie in the mirror like he'd taught me on my twenty-first birthday. And there he is—the heart-shaped face and Chambers nose. I find his socks and worn, lace-up shoes. I draw on his rabbit-fur lined gloves, shift into the good overcoat and Irish tweed cap. I will be warm in winter. I will check the oil and antifreeze. If my battery dies, I'll know what to do, which is the grounding cable, which supplies the juice. I could never catch my father on camera, only images of him disappearing, the sliding door in its aluminum groove. PVCs won't hurt you, they told the workers, that plutonium, those clouds of DDT that children played in like lawn sprinklers. All filmed by Dow in black and white.

He absorbed it daily through skin. Asbestos fibers, floating isotopes, he labored faithfully, believing. He breathed it in. Landscapes cut through with highways hand-laid, like a pyramid. Architecture from his fingers whose bones dissolved inside their sheaths of skin.

I carry my father with me—his pocket knife, his good white shirts. I drive his pickup with the rusted fenders, explore its sun-blanched interior for signs he left behind. Receipts. Manuals. Beneath the vinyl seat, I retrieve his homemade car scent. No pine-shaped deodorant board, but—and I remember the gray, mid-winter morning he made it—a Florida orange, studded and fragrant with cloves.

Promised Candy

A DECADE FROM NOW, when everyone works either for Starbucks or Time Warner, when George W. Bush has been coronated king, I'll be down South in a compound like David Koresh or Jim Jones. Except my followers will be nomadic cats who smoke burly-wood pipes and tattered dogs who never get dental checkups and my religion will be horticulture—carrots, sweet corn and bush beans called Kentucky Wonders. I will sit cross-legged in the garden and watch the sunset flare un-natural but gorgeous colors like a Duraflame log, which burns for hours, consuming itself without an ash. I will talk to my father.

What I really want to say is that I miss my father's vegetable beef soup. Always a potful, or brown beans with corn bread fried in a cast-iron skillet. Plenty. Always made sure we had something good to eat. Not Mom. Her basic food groups: Sara Lee cinnamon wedges, drip grind coffee, Jack Daniel's and Kent cigarettes gathering in ashes as long as a philosopher's forefinger.

My Dad ate his soup in the den watching Rush Limbaugh, didn't like the look of the dentures that student at the medical center made for him. He'd been so handsome, strong, built half the houses in town. He dined privately now, then came out to where my mother and I talked at the cherry dining room table and repeated everything Rush said, wheezing with laughter. Rush's jokes hit him like a two-by-four.

My mother would fire rebuttals while she scanned the seed catalogues. Black tulips from Holland, purple string beans and blue potatoes. She could defeat Rush Limbaugh without a pause in her page turning and that was the reason he did it, to hear that back talk, to rile us. To him, this was a good time. This was conversation. There was no malicious intent when he said:

I have to go meet one of my "secretaries" now ...

I have to go to a militia meeting at Ruby Ridge ...

I'm expecting Monica Lewinsky at three ...

Just tell her to wait in the den ...

What I really want to say is that I shopped for bones in Star Market in Cambridge, beef bones sawed with a sharp blade on a January day so cold spit froze in the air and wind boomeranged words back into my mouth, burned my skin like a flatiron.

Though I am vegetarian, I bought four bones, which I roasted while sautéing onions, carrots and mushrooms in the big Dutch oven. I de-glazed the bones with good red wine from Italy, added it to the soup along with herbs, chopped tomatoes, barley, simmered it for a few hours to let the flavors blend, carried it to the new house and fed the carpenters.

What I really want to say is that I don't know who I am anymore. I have reabsorbed like mist into the ocean, shattered like the window in the witch's house, the one made of purple candy. I never knew how fragile, how brittle, how easily lost. I carry the loss like cotton candy spun with pink light in my chest. Insubstantial. Instead of heart meat, lungs like bag pipes. I feel the hollow when I trail after someone leaving in the snow. Please don't go.

A hole like a hollow-nosed bullet through the third chakra, the solar plexus, the sun, the self. Hollow-nosed, small at the entrance, blow your whole back out. I fall into the deep, cold sky, searching for my father in a blue star. I will ask him questions. *What would you do, Dad?* and he'll say, *Stand up for yourself. You don't have to take any crap. Tell them all to go to hell.* I've seen my father crawl up a man like a panther, my five-seven father, up a six-three man, because he'd stuck by the man, bailed him out of jail, given him a job, seen him through, and he didn't like to be betrayed the way the man done him.

My father's absence, a betrayal too, Death is an absence I am bound to forgive. He'd always been remote, seemed closer now, in the bone marrow, the recipes written in blue ball-point on yellow legal pads. In the seed packets that arrived in February, square, colorful spread across the cherry dining room table like candy promised to a little girl.

Blue Land

.

I'VE HAD A REAL BAD DAY, Blue half-whispers into the telephone.

I hold the phone in my right hand, my left hand on my chest to slow my heartbeat; 3:47 according to the square red numerals on my bedside clock. I'm always glad to hear from Blue, even if it is the middle of the night.

"Well, mine's not been exactly coconut cream pie." I shift in the bed to rearrange the ankle I'd sprained on my first day at Dynabody.

"You've still got your sheriff up there in Vance, don't you?" Blue asks.

I admit that we do and listen as Blue describes in detail how Trigg County had lost theirs. She explains that one of her clients had been summoned to court by his daughter. Oh, *she'd* put up with it for years, the daughter said in the deposition, but when the old man started in on *her* daughter, his own grandbaby, well she'd had enough.

"At the trial," Blue says, pausing while I set the scene in my mind. "My client sensed the wind was not blowing in his favor." I hear a watery sound, probably Blue pouring another glass of wine. "During the prosecutor's cross-examination, my client leaped over the courthouse rail and snatched up the little Nester boy, who didn't have the sense to run. He used the boy as hostage till he could drive off in his pickup. When the sheriff caught up with my client out in Rocky Branch, the old man dispatched the sheriff with a shotgun right there on the hillside, face down in a patch of lady slippers. I'm glad Dad isn't around to see all this stuff."

I am sitting up in bed now, my ankle propped on a pillow. "What about the little Nester boy?"

"Oh, he's a celebrity. Everybody in town's been bringing him ice cream," Blue says. "Can you hang on a minute?"

I wait a good five minutes before I hear Blue's footsteps returning to the phone. I hear the whisk of a striking match and a sharp inhale, either Marlboro or Appalachian Gold.

"Remember these?" Blue says, exhaling. She reads three Millay sonnets in a row, then a few paragraphs from a short story by Alice Munro.

Blue's soft mountain voice always sounded like music to me. I listen as the sky pales to indigo out my bedroom window.

Blue interrupts herself mid-sentence to ask me a question I've heard before. "Ruby, why was it so ... intense?"

"I don't know," I answer. "Maybe because it was so dangerous."

The only time Blue ever admits anything happened between us is when she is either very drunk or stoned.

"You'll come see me soon, won't you?"

"You think it's a shorter trip to whatever holler you're living in, than you driving to Vance to see me?" My ankle aches under its brown paper and vinegar wrap, a remedy my father had taught me.

"You missed my forty-fifth birthday," she says, trumping me.

Blue doesn't remember her forty-fifth birthday because she drank so much wine and sat out in her arbor with glow-lites and a bee hive with real honey-bees and a fountain connected to a garden hose. She calls it Blue Land. Kinda like Graceland. Kinda like Dollywood.

Blue's a public defender who lives in Hazard, Kentucky. She's had two sons, two abortions and one real girlfriend, yours truly, Ruby Chambers. Her elder son, JJ—they've all got nicknames like that down in Hazard, Uncle AI or Cousin CR—designed to deflect attention from their real names. Take Blue's father, GB, Goliath Bush, or Blue herself, Bertha Eloise, names passed down with gnarled-handed tenacity from a bygone time when, I guess, people hadn't heard of modern names yet, and therefore did not consider carrying Martha Maybelline or Lester Methuselah their whole lives a particular cross to bear.

Blue's son JJ (Jarrad Josiah) is a dead ringer for her first husband, a former quarterback for the Trigg County Cougars. Blond and square, a quarterback and prettier than Blue. She was the smart one, valedictorian, editor of the school paper.

Somebody fixed them up their junior year of high school and they've been arguing ever since.

When Blue eased her suitcases down on the linoleum floor of room 315 of Jewel Hall the first day of our freshman year, I thought she was the homeliest girl I'd ever seen. Squat and sallow-skinned, chipmunk-cheeked and limp-haired, nothing to rest your gaze on, except for a pair of extraordinary lips, well-formed and full, the deep scarlet of the good cordial my grandfather made from blackberries.

I felt indignant at not having been paired up with someone more talkative and cheerful. Afternoons, I watched crossly as she slumped into her bed after classes, napping till the quarterback rang for her. I decided that Blue and I had nothing in common except couture. From the first day of class, we'd both worn jeans, saddle oxfords and T-shirts with the names of any university other than our own printed across the front. I assumed the motive for her easygoing dress was the same as mine, blessed relief from the past twelve years of dresses with anklets, Villager skirts with matching cable-knit sweaters and nylon hose. I never asked her directly, though. In the first few months of sharing the same twelve-by-twelve room, we'd barely exchanged two sentences.

One evening Blue flopped down across from me in the cafeteria and struck a match on the bottom of one of her saddle oxfords. She lit a Marlboro and flicked out the flame.

"I heard they put saltpeter on the mashed potatoes here," she said, French-inhaling the smoke. "You know, to keep the students' sex drive down."

I lay my fork gently on the waxed table cloth. "Like in the

army," I said, staring at her perfect cherry lips. "Where's the quarterback?"

"Practice," she said and blew a couple of smoke rings. "Wanna take a drive out to The Clock?"

Paris, Kentucky, is a dry town, so local bootleggers kept irregular hours in a concrete-block building on the outskirts of town that used to belong to a watch maker. Within an hour we were back in our dorm room sipping sherry from miniature mugs that read *Skol!* and *Salut!*

Maybe we were more alike than I'd thought, this Blue and I, in our bell-bottoms and black turtlenecks, interested only in literature and theater classes, lonely yet preferring to be burned at the stake rather than rushing for a sorority.

By Thanksgiving, we were meeting after class to experiment with local restaurants and writing arbitrary poetry in our dormitory room. First, Blue composed a line then folded the paper down so I was forced to write my line blind. By the end of the accordioned page, we'd produced something we considered very fine.

She read me poems, retold stories from books and plays: *The Dollmaker, The Stranger, The Scarlet Letter.* She spun terrifying hill legends till my hands trembled from cold. I'd never seen such a somber expression lodged so deeply in a pair of eyes.

"Love is not all," Blue read from Millay's *Collected Poems* till I fell asleep on the thin dormitory mattress. *Love is not meat nor drink nor shelter from the rain ...*

Blue nicknamed the boys I dated—Santa Claus, because of the boy's flyaway platinum hair, my Fruity Lab Partner who had, Blue claimed, an extra row of pointy teeth around his regular teeth, like a shark. "One kiss could be lethal," she warned.

She was hardest on my steady boyfriend, Fury, whose real name was Dennis, but who looked to Blue like the television horse. "He's a pathological liar," Blue claimed. "He's never been to college or he wouldn't have to brag about it. He doesn't sing in a rock band, either. Can you imagine? *Neigh, neigh, whinny.*"

I watched as Blue collapsed backward on the bed laughing at her own joke. It was true, Dennis did look like a horse, a sleek, handsome, toothy horse. I was beginning to find Blue's post-date cross-examinations more exciting than the dates.

Blue dated only the quarterback, except on occasional weekends when they were broken up. Then we'd go to fraternity parties and dance under fluorescent lights or hippie parties with black lights where Janis Joplin sang *Piece of My Heart.* We chewed bits of paper with purple stains on them called microdots.

One night we took mescaline with a boy we thought looked like John Lennon. I watched him toss a fortune-telling eight ball while I was peaking on the drug. His arm rose, snatched the ball from the air, pitched it up again. I could follow every movement separately, like time-lapse photography.

"Traces," he said, letting me know the lingo for my hallucinations. He upended the ball and read the message as it floated up in the murky water. "Yes, definitely," he said, smiling at me with teeth as square as Scrabble tiles.

Back in our dorm we carved peanuts and cashews to look like John Lennon and Fury and the terrifying Tom Sharp from our Oral Interpretation class, setting them along the window ledge to be admired or snacked on.

Every afternoon, I rushed upstairs to peer down from our third-floor window as my secret crush, Dan Gram, continued to his dorm after dropping me off at Jewel Hall. His black hair waved over the wool collar of his navy peacoat. When we walked together, he looked straight ahead and spoke in a neutral way that I found mysterious and compelling.

"He's a gram of a man," Blue sang from her bed. She seemed so soft, her body utterly casual in her frayed sweat suit.

She looked over my shoulder, down at the top of Dan Gram's disappearing head.

"Cute, right?" I said.

"You're so indiscriminate," she said.

I felt winded, as though she'd sucker punched me. But I didn't care about Dan Gram. Not really.

It was November and the room had grown dark in the time I'd stood staring out the window. The hallway light streaming over the transom haloed Blue's silky brown hair as it fell forward onto her face. I noticed the outline of her lips, that could form perfect O's of smoke rings. I wondered if those lips would be softer, sweeter than a boy's if I kissed them.

In the lobby of Jewel Hall, vinyl couches and chairs formed a square with the check-in counter for ten P.M. curfew. An adjoining room contained nab and soft drink machines, which Blue was always feeding quarters, even though she wasn't supposed to have sugar. There was a communal ironing board in there, too, and a long table with folding chairs for card-playing or meetings of the radical SDS. I'm not sure which room

Blue chose when she intercepted Fury the day he brought me the engagement ring. I didn't see Fury after that and I never laid eyes on the ring. When I asked Blue what happened, she said for me to never mind.

I'd accepted from the beginning that Blue was in charge, but I wondered if she'd said more to Fury about the two of us than she'd ever said to me. Neither Blue nor I mentioned that our arm wrestling had transformed into hand-holding under our winter coats at movies. We'd begun to set the alarm for five A.M. so we could get into separate beds before our dorm mother ducked her head in random doors for room check.

I didn't miss Fury or Santa Claus or Fruity Lab Partner. I wasn't even bothered by our classmates who'd begun whispering when we walked through the lobby or passed by them on Maybrook Street on our way to class.

I felt fortified inside the universe Blue and I created together, armed by her wit and self-possession. The quarterback must have felt the same way, buoyed by association into a territory neither of us could have conceived without her. I hoped that Blue did not view the quarterback and me in the same light; a boy so naive that once, when driving her home from the hospital after a diabetic relapse, she persuaded him to buy her a six-pack of soda, telling him that strawberry pop counted as fruit.

As a public defender, Blue needs to stop herself from dreaming about her clients; so she has made very good friends with Ernest and Julio Gallo. She wanted to be a poet, not a lawyer, but her father needed a son to follow in his tracks as Hazard's county attorney. He once told Blue that he knew what her friend Ruby Chambers was, but his daughter was certainly not one. He had to hold his head up in this town. Blue defends men who molest their daughters, who slash their wives' tires and faces when they get angry. "How can you stand to do that?" I once asked her about a locally famous case of a woman's body found in a freezer. "They deserve a defense," she'd answered. "But, did he do it?" I asked. Her glare answered me. *Of course he did it.* Blue has a lot to drink about.

Most novels about girls who fall into each other's arms end in radical separation or death. Sometimes the lovers are just expelled from the girl's school: *And then I never saw Teresa, I never saw Antonia, I never saw Jenine, again.* I've always found these endings careless and cheap, as though the whole gravity of forever could be encapsulated and swallowed like a tab of darkness. The thing is, you usually do see the person again, even if the movie you imagined yourselves starring in turns out bad.

I didn't end our dream easily, the one where Blue and I boarded a Greyhound in front of DeJarnette's Drugs, rode to South Dakota and raised blueberries. I was seventeen and had no strategy, so I just gave her the straight stuff: begging annoyed her, crying made her lose respect, judgment made her silent. It had to end somewhere.

The summer after our freshman year, Blue threw a party on her father's houseboat. I tried one last time, easing into the bunk beside her, sliding an arm around her waist. She pushed my hand definitively away and said viciously, loud enough to wake the sleepers, "Stop."

I lay there in humiliated silence the remaining hours of that night, the weight of her refusal pressing against my breast bone. The next morning I drove the two hours home to Vance listening to Stevie Wonder sing *Place in the Sun* where there was *hope for everyone* from the radio of my Firebird and it did feel like those stories I hated, like beginning the process of never hearing from her again.

But like I said, you usually do see the person again and you feel the same way or you don't. Or maybe you've realized it wasn't them anyway, that it was your mother or part of yourself that you're afraid of, or were trying to kill. Blue tried hard to kill it.

She got pregnant with the quarterback during their last fling for old time's sake. "I can't believe you're going to marry the quarterback," I said from the phone in my apartment near the campus of the university where I'd transferred. The quarterback and Blue returned to our old campus and lived two blocks from Jewel Hall, in the married dorm called, no lie, Normal Hall.

When Blue was in law school and pregnant with her second child, I received a note from her in the mail: *I'm pregnant. Not the quarterback. Love, Blue.*

It was the slow season in the book business, so I drove my van up to her apartment in Cincinnati. I spent the week scrubbing dishes and pans caked with some kind of glossy orange substance that had to be pried off with a screwdriver. I gathered up a trunkful of empty quart beer bottles to redeem for a nickel each.

Every morning, Blue woke JJ, who'd just turned five, by snapping on the hundred watt overhead in his room and clapping her hands, which always made him cry. Every night, she stirred up a dish of Hamburger or Tuna Helper. Then she started in on her quarts.

It's a mystery to me how she ever got her law degree, passed her bar exams and got herself to the hospital to bear her second son, Alonzo Zaragoza, a dark-skinned child with blond surfer-boy hair whom everyone calls Ziggy.

Antonio's Pizza and Daddy-O's Diner are the only real restaurants still open in Hazard. If you want to have something besides the Colonel's crispy strips or a Wendy's Thick and Frosty, then you have to go downtown. Blue's office building is flanked by the Army/Navy store on one side and Antonio's Pizza on the other. Every weekday, Blue orders a pizza with pepperonis scorched to little rounds of charcoal, large iced tea no sugar, and two lemon wedges.

Her office is on the second floor of one of the formerly prestigious colonial-style brick buildings. Even though Blue's father has passed away, the smoked glass door still has LINVILLE & LINVILLE ATTORNEYS-AT-LAW stenciled in a gold-and-black arc just like in *Chinatown*.

There used to be money in Hazard, back when there was still coal to strip mine, then, after that, a whole generation of lawyers, including Blue's daddy, who got rich on the black-lung suits. Now, there is nothing left but some reclaimed hillsides planted in trees and excavated hillsides of furrowed red dirt sliding into the river. That, and vast fields of sorghum cane.

All summer, Blue goes to work in cut-offs and T-shirts that tout such phrases as TEAM REDNECK and TONYA HARDING FOR PRESIDENT. She's wears flip-flops, not the good kind they make nowadays, but the totally flat kind that come all in a bin at the dime store. You have to pinch your toes together just to keep them on your feet. Over the summer, they soften and erode till they fall apart. That's how Blue looks now as she glances up from her desk: worn down and soft, her voice whispery, her shoulder-length hair, though permed, surrendering its curls to the humidity.

I wait for her in the Army/Navy store while she finishes some paperwork. I browse among shelves of shotgun shells, home-canned pickle relish and gingham bonnets. The knife case houses a good selection of Case XX, bone-handled Bokers and a special velvet-boxed edition of a hunting knife with *Remember Waco* stamped on its 8-inch blade.

Early September can be Kentucky's hottest month and it must be sorghum harvesting time, because when I step out of the Army/Navy Store onto the sidewalk, the wild, rich scent of fresh cut cane saturates the breeze as it moseys through town.

Blue lives at the end of a lane with a neighbor who keeps dogs by the dozen in cages in her back yard. "'Rescues,' she calls them," Blue says, as her all-terrain vehicle earns its keep on the gouged gravel road.

It's twilight by the time we settle in to the lawn chairs by the beehives and the makeshift fountain. Blue plugs a string of Christmas lights into an orange extension cord and the trees and bushes glow in colors around us.

"Blue Land," she says and hands me a goblet of chilled white wine.

"Where's Ziggy?" I ask.

"Oh, him." Blue shrugs. "He's not allowed in my house anymore." Blue eases herself all the way back on the full-length chaise and drinks wine like she is thirsty. Her theory about why Ziggy went off his rocker can be summed up in one word—pot. Pot made him put his fists through her doors, rip them off their hinges. Pot made him throw her refrigerator off the front porch and into her tomato plants. The last time she let him in, he stole her television and DVD player. His brother JJ tried to straighten him out, but she thought he'd just plain gone crazy. "JJ too, since we're on the subject of my offspring."

I'd once heard the Linville family described as the little Mafia of Hazard. I assumed that meant they were at least loyal to one another, and maybe at one time they had been.

"Ziggy lives in a tent somewhere in the mountains," Blue says, tilting her head toward the dark rise beyond her barbed wire fence. "I have to keep my doors locked." Blue refills her half-full glass with wine. I'd seen my dad use the same trick to hide how much he was drinking from my mother. The wine tastes like one part liquid Jell-O, two parts Mennen Skin Bracer.

"Ever hear from your old beau Dan Gram?" Blue asks.

"Once I figured out you were jealous of my boyfriends," I say, "that explained a lot."

"I was not jealous," Blue says, swatting away a stray honey bee. "He was a gram of a man," she sings like she used to when I watched him from the dormitory window.

"He was six-four," I say. "That's over a gram."

Blue's chair squeals faintly when she shifts to look at me. "You never cared about me. Just old Dan Gram."

I sip my wine as the name resonates, then decays into silence. "Maybe that's just the lie you tell yourself." I am teasing. I am serious as God on Judgment Day.

And here we are again, not ten minutes into our visit and already up against the wall of our opposing versions of the past. How Blue was smarter, though I was more clever. How Blue left me high and dry, how I wouldn't have been faithful to her anyway.

Blue fishes in her back pocket, then hands me two pictures. "You're not going to believe these."

In the colored lights from the trees, I can make out an image of myself with long sun-streaked hair, ragged jeans and a beige army officer's shirt. The other one is of Blue with cat-eye glasses, a denim jacket and corduroy bell-bottoms.

"We were just a couple of kids!" I say, shocked.

"I know," Blue makes a hushed, collapsing sound intended to be laughter. "We thought we were so cool. You know, I did run into Dan Gram a few months ago, down here to take some insurance depositions. He was having a Hot Brown for lunch over at Daddy-O's."

A Hot Brown is an oversized, open-faced sandwich, with two inches of sliced turkey, crisscrossed by bacon strips, deluged by white sauce, then the whole thing sealed in a crust of melted cheddar. Dan Gram must be huge by now. Huge and greasy and working on his second heart attack.

"He asked about you," Blue says. "Did you know he and his friends called us the blue-ankle twins? Because we didn't wear socks in the dead of winter. Plus, we always prowled around outside, away from everyone."

"So they noticed," I say. "Even though you always had a boyfriend."

Blue stares up into the trees. "The blue-ankle twins. That's us."

It is the hill habit to cover things up with euphemism. Nobody ever called Blue's dad a big fat alcoholic slob, they just called him a big man. We aren't sitting in the ramshackle yard of a self-destructive closet case who'd damaged both her sons beyond repair. We're in Blue Land.

I pour my glass full of Blue's bad wine and try to pick up the threads of the story she is telling. I watch her lips form their drawn-out vowels and lazy consonants. After all this time, those lips could still stir me.

Blue ricochets between stories—clients, friends, people who've been dead for two hundred years, characters in novels and old rock songs. Hazard seems to have more than its share of men with women's names—Shirley, Carol, Lacy; and women with men's names—Michael, Scott, Miller. Couples where you couldn't tell who was who. Carol and Sally, Polly and Ellie, Billy and Marty.

It almost sounds like the hills are full of old gay couples who come out at only night, like Blue's son or the ghosts that roamed these hills in the rising mist, like dreams you yearned for but could never make come true. All tangible at night, all evaporating in the dawn.

"I may have always had a boyfriend," Blue says, pointing a shaky forefinger at me. "But you've always had mistresses."

"We've been broken up for twenty-five years," I say. "Remember?"

"I remember," she says, her voice a little bleary with alcohol. The dogs howling from their cages sound mournful and lonesome as wolves. "You know, Ruby, not everybody's strong enough to be queer."

The word hung in the air, menacing as a drove of honeybees hovering in the dark. That's what we'd called it the first time, when she'd climbed into my bunk, silently so as not to wake our roommates.

I hadn't known back then how words could be hooks that lasted forever. If you fessed up, if you refused to deny, if you *made a point of it*, well they'd have to tar and feather you; they'd have to disown you; they'd have to hunt you down. So they just called Blue peculiar, a loner, Bertha Eloise Linville, GB's daughter, little blue-ankle girl, little Blue. In a town like Hazard, nicknames can be your salvation.

Acknowledgments

Grateful acknowledgment is made to the editors of the following publications in which some of these stories have appeared: *StoryQuarterly, Imagine International Journal, Wind, The Louisville Review, South Dakota Review, Salamander, The Pennsylvania Review, Primavera, Provincetown Magazine,* and *Phoebe.*

Sín Verqüenza first appeared, in a different form, in *Salamander.*

Many thanks to my wonderful mentor and to the Brookline writing group for their warm hearts and unsparing eyes.

Thanks also to The Writers' Room of Boston, the St. Botolph Club, Wellspring House, and the Duxbury Writers' Colony for their support of my work.

Special thanks to the Polyho editorial board and adjuncts for their many talents, generosity and expertise.

I am grateful to my friends and family in my urban Massachusetts home and my rural Kentucky home, for helping shuttle me back and forth and welcoming me into their circles of light.

Thanks to Jimmy Robinson and Ray Oney, who ensure safe haven in my old Kentucky home, and to Jutta Kausch and Avery Rimer, for their wisdom and guidance as I learn to apply Ray's pithy advice: "Get your head on, girl."

Deep gratitude to James Blandini, Robin Marlowe, Danny Marcus, Aquaman, and Dr. Pamela Wine.

"We really are movie stars."